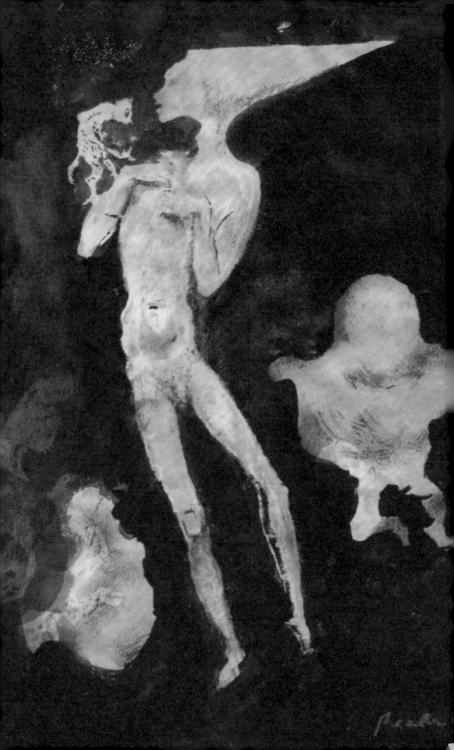

Boy in Darkness
and Other Stories

Boy in Darkness and Other Stories

MERVYN PEAKE

EDITED BY Sebastian Peake
WITH A FOREWORD BY Joanne Harris

Peter Owen Publishers
London and Chicago

PETER OWEN PUBLISHERS
20 Holland Park Avenue
London W11 3QU

Peter Owen books are distributed in the USA and Canada by
Independent Publishers Group/Trafalgar Square
814 North Franklin Street, Chicago, IL 60610, USA

First published in Great Britain by Peter Owen Publishers 2007
Reprinted 2011

'Boy in Darkness' first published in *Sometime, Never: Three Tales of Imagination* by William Golding, John Wyndham and Mervyn Peake, Eyre and Spottiswoode, London, 1956
'The Weird Journey' first published in *Harvest, Volume 1: Travel*, edited by Vincent Stuart, Castle Press, London, 1948
'I Bought a Palm-tree' first published in a corrected version in *Peake's Progress*, Allen Lane, London, 1978
'The Connoisseurs' first published in *Lilliput*, January 1950, Vol. 26, No. 1, Issue No. 151, pp. 58–9
'Danse Macabre' first published in *Science Fantasy*, 1963, Vol. 21, No. 61, pp. 46–55
'Same Time, Same Place' first published in *Science Fantasy*, 1963, Vol. 20, No. 60, pp. 57–65

ISBN 978-0-7206-1389-6

A catalogue record for this book is available from the British Library

Designed by Benedict Richards
Printed and bound by CPI Antony Rowe

Acknowledgements

SEBASTIAN PEAKE

FOLLOWING THE SUGGESTION that a new edition of short stories by my late father be published as a collection, I turned to various friends, family members and collectors of his work for assistance. Peter Winnington, *éminence grise* on the subject of Mervyn Peake, pointed out that the text of the first edition of the novella *Boy in Darkness*, published in 1956, was the one most free from the errors found in subsequent editions, a fact otherwise likely to have been missed; while my brother Fabian and sister Clare offered their own invaluable and considered views on the selection of drawings to be included. The collector and gallery owner Chris Beetles was kind enough to allow a number of drawings owned by him to be reproduced, and Alison Eldred, who offered her thoughts on further images, greatly helped with their reproduction. Joanne Harris's sensitive introduction eloquently captures the spirit of the writer with her perceptive observations on the stories. Finally, I am indebted to Peter Owen Publishers for accepting the idea of combining the stories with previously unpublished drawings and other illustrations, thus making available two aspects of my father's art in one volume, and especially to Antonia Owen, Nick Pearson and Benedict Richards for all their hard work on the production of the book.

Foreword

JOANNE HARRIS

MOST READERS WILL know of Mervyn Peake first and fore-most as the author of the acclaimed Titus books: *Titus Groan*, *Gormenghast* and *Titus Alone*. Some may be familiar with his astonishingly prolific work as an illustrator, which ranges from char-coal drawings of tremendous energy and oils reminiscent of early Picasso to delicate pen-and ink illustrations not unlike the work of Beardsley. Some may have read his war poetry or his surreal comic verse, similar in so many ways to the work of Edward Lear or Lewis Carroll. In fact, the sheer breadth of Peake's creativity can be almost daunting to the reader, drawing as it does from such a diverse palette as to almost defy classification, every piece of the Peake puzzle hinting at a new and different facet of the man's almost limitless imagination.

These six short stories, published together for the first time, may be enjoyed in a number of ways; first as wonderful tales in their own right, or as a series of exercises in different styles, but mostly as a fascinating glance into the workings of the writer's mind, a series of snapshots taken during the course of one man's extraordinary life.

'The Weird Journey' is a playful exploration of what Baudelaire calls *Correspondances*; the secret, quasi-mystical connections between the senses. In this story Peake plays with the language of colour and form to create a Dalí-like vista across which the narrator travels, cata-loguing in the most minute detail the nightmarish images that emerge along the way.

'The Connoisseurs', with its brittle dialogue and satirical view of the art scene, reads uncannily like a snippet from one of Oscar Wilde's short plays. 'Danse Macabre' takes a familiar image from the traditional Gothic tale and gives it a new and sinister twist, while 'Same Time, Same Place' was inspired, albeit unwittingly, by a lady who shared a table with the Peakes at Lyons Corner House, and it shows how easily the author was able to assimilate aspects of mundane life into his fan-tasy, giving them a new and bizarre complexion.

Humorous and self-deprecating, 'I Bought A Palm-tree' records an incident in the life of the Peake family during their time on Sark and gives a welcome glimpse of the light-hearted, whimsical side of the author's personality.

But it is *Boy in Darkness*, the most complex and perhaps the best known of Peake's short works, that stands out as the masterpiece in this collection. Like much of his fiction, it takes place in a kind of Freudian twilight midway between reality and dream. A young and rebellious Boy – who, though unnamed, bears many similarities to the youthful Titus Groan – escapes the hated confines of his ancestral home and the stifling layers of ritual that immobilize it and escapes into the surround-ing wasteland, where he falls into the beastly hands of the vile, bullying Hyena and the cringing, unsettling Goat; once men who have been long ago transformed into animal parodies of themselves by their blind and fearsome master, the Lamb.

This Kafkaesque tale has been variously interpreted as a Freudian fable of emerging sexuality, a coming-of-age story, an indictment on organized religion and a satire on Nazism, but in the end, with the rest of Peake's work, it defies easy categorization. Lurid, brooding and sinister, it shares with the Titus books (to which it is undoubtedly related) a peculiar richness and sensuality; a vivid awareness of the small details of sound, colour, scent and shape that gives the author's work its tremendous emotional impact as well as its enduring appeal.

Visually, it might take the form of the darkest, grimmest of puppet-shows; the grotesque half-animal characters, the mannered dialogue and the theatrical nature of the setting would seem to place this story in the realm of distant fantasy. And yet the Boy's quasi-existential struggle against the dreadful magnetism of the Lamb and his unwelcome gift of metamorphosis still holds a peculiar resonance in a world increasingly at odds with itself, and Peake's spirited depiction of the inarticulate, instinctive rebellion of youth – against authority, against tradition, even against its own roots – is as convincing now as it was sixty years ago.

Because, though the richness of Peake's language and the breadth of his imagination never fail to impress, it is the writer's emotional range that secures his position among the great storytellers of the twentieth century. These stories reflect this temperament; six very different views of the world among the countless mental landscapes drawn by this most mercurial of visionaries.

Preface

SEBASTIAN PEAKE

CHRISTMAS WAS THE time of year when my father would invite the family to gather round the open fire in our sitting-room to hear his latest ghost story. By the flickering light of the crackling logs we would wait for him to begin.

Shadows cast by the flames would take on lives and shapes of their own and add to our anticipation, while the stories themselves never failed to send shudders down our spines. Before he started the story he would sometimes ask us to suggest how we'd describe the outlines thrown up by the firelight on the ceiling and walls. A tree, perhaps, a mountain peak, a sword, a witch's hat? we'd venture. He would offer a suggestion or two of his own and impress us with the aptness of his observations.

And then the story would begin Each time we'd be lulled into a false sense of security by his soft, mellifluous voice, but before long the narrative would develop into a tale as hair-raising and frightening as the previous time. We had been lured deep into the chasms of his limitless imagination, while we awaited the denouement with a mixture of captivation and apprehension.

As the tale unfolded, my father would lay false trails, giving the impression that we might, for once, have guessed the outcome, but as

we listened, transfixed and rigid with excitement, we found that, once again, we had got it wrong. Little by little he had worked his usual magic and enticed us ever more cleverly into his creation until a point was reached when the tension in the room was such that only with its conclusion would we be able to relax. The story having reached its chilling and dramatic climax, the lights in the room would be turned on once more . . .

In the following selection of stories, never before collected in one volume, the reader is invited to experience some of the sensations my father could evoke through his writing, and, as the painterly composition of his words unfolds on the page, the anticipation we children experienced – as well as the satisfaction induced by a tale well told – might once more be experienced. Accompanying the stories are a range of his paintings and illustrations, created as much for pleasure as were the stories that he crafted so skilfully.

Included here is one of my favourites, 'I Bought a Palm-tree', a tale that evokes in me a vivid memory not only of my father's desire to plant such a tree in the garden of our home on Sark, in the Channel Islands, but also of what lies buried beneath its roots.

Given permission by one of the teachers at my Guernsey boarding-school to explore a German arms dump, hidden ingeniously behind a hinged boulder in the rock face of a cliff on the island, a few lucky boys were allowed to help themselves to the weapons revealed within. My treasured haul included a ceremonial dagger, a Luger pistol, a helmet and a swastika-embossed sword. A few weeks later, after learning about the incident, the island police contacted the school and requested that everything removed from the cave be handed in. But by then I had already hidden my cache, where it remains to this day!

Illustrations

The drawings, sketches and paintings included in this book were created by Mervyn Peake at different periods of his life and have been selected by his children, Sebastian, Fabian and Clare, to enhance the story *Boy in Darkness* and the other pieces in this collection. None was originally intended by the artist specifically to accompany or illustrate these particular stories. The picture on page 18 shows the front cover, with a drawing by the author, of the first edition of the novel *Gormenghast*, published by Eyre and Spottiswoode in London in 1950. The illustration on page 19 is a sketch showing Flay and Titus in front of the doors of Swelter's great kitchen drawn by Peake in 1951 as a preliminary design for a proposed opera adapted from the Titus trilogy, with music by Benjamin Britten. The drawing on page 108 is a detail from an illustration from *Captain Slaughterboard Drops Anchor*, published by Eyre and Spottiswoode in London in 1945.

Contents

Foreword to *Boy in Darkness*

MAEVE GILMORE

I N 1956 MY husband Mervyn Peake was commissioned to write a long short story for a book with the projected title of *Sometime, Never*. There were also contributions by two other authors: William Golding with a story about the past called *Envoy Extraordinary* and John Wyndham with *Consider Her Ways* which was about the future. Mervyn's contribution was *Boy in Darkness* and had a sub-title 'The Dream'.

The publishers, apart from stipulating the approximate length of the stories, for the obvious reason of making the finished book a balanced whole, gave free rein to the authors to write or create whatever each one wished. So there was the whole world to choose from, and the world of the imagination, tempered with observation from the world which we know around us, gave birth to *Boy in Darkness*.

At one time my husband had had the idea of writing stories of episodes in the life of Titus, hero of three of his novels, which do not take place in his books *Titus Groan*, *Gormenghast* and *Titus Alone*, for no book, however long, can possibly chronicle every incident in its character's life. There are many events, and adventures or meetings with people, that happen outside the book, just as we, however close we are to our families or friends, can only know a small part of what makes up other people's lives.

So that in thinking of the story which he was about to write, he put this idea into practice, and, though the boy in *Boy in Darkness* is assuredly Titus Groan, he does not call him so by name.

The Boy has just celebrated his fourteenth birthday. In the novel *Gormenghast* Titus reaches adolescence, which coincides in time with what was happening in the story. Titus had an urgent longing to break loose from the fetters of his circumscribed life in the castle where he was a prisoner of ritual 'the meaning of which had long been forgotten', and in common with all youth he was searching for adventure . . .

to be alone in a land where nothing can be recognized, that is what he feared, and that is what he longed for. For what is exploration without peril?

. . . There came the upsurge again! The thrill and speculation of escape. Of escape to where? And when? *When* should it be? 'Why now! now! now!' came the voice. 'Be up and be gone. What are you waiting for?'

And so, with no backward looking and no forward planning he left his vast home in search of adventure, alone.

To be able to join the Boy in his adventure you must read the story not only with your mind but with your eyes and with your ears, sharing the sights and sounds with him, almost as though you are following him with a film camera. For it is described very vividly, and, though for certain the reader may not have seen or heard or experienced such events, in some cases they are extensions of our own experience.

The hounds which are described early on in the story sprang from an eerie walk my husband and I had in France in the Auvergne. It was a dark and oppressively still night, and we were walking on an isolated road, when we came to some very high, massive wrought-iron gates which led to a rather desolate château. Alongside the road, stretching for many miles it seemed, loomed a stone wall, higher still. As we

approached the gates, in the silence and the gloom we were aware of many jostling shapes attempting to leap them and the sound of angry panting and frustrated yelping. As we walked by the side of the wall the creatures on the other side kept pace with us, keeping up their malevolent chase. That sound and the feeling of fear it engendered remained for many years, until it was transformed into the hounds who gathered themselves in a half-moon and urged the Boy eastwards to the bank of the great river.

The adventure which the Boy has embarked on leads him into a frightening world, and he is afraid and filled with a 'disembodied pain, an illness so penetrating, so horrible, that had he been given the opportunity to die he would have taken it. No normal sensation could find a way through this overpowering nausea of the soul that filled him.' But he is resourceful, and he feels that he can outwit the two grotesque creatures Goat and Hyena who have captured him. He realizes the fear in which they live of the Lamb, with his insatiable lust for power, which he learns has been exercised not only on them but on countless unknown beings, for centuries, in the subterranean mines. He knows that he needs more than resourcefulness to combat the blind Lamb, but by flattery and coercion he attempts to rally Goat and Hyena to his side to destroy the malevolent Lamb.

The story ends bravely for the Boy, and he escapes back to the banks of the wide river where the hounds awaited him.

Is it a dream? Is it a nightmare? Is it true? What does it mean?

It was written as a story, to be read as a story, but many interpretations have been given to it. Some people read it for itself alone and enjoy or not the unfolding of the frightening adventure. Others have seen a religious significance in it, or others the desolation of our world destroyed, and even some a descent into the blackness of man's soul where his deepest fears are hidden. It is all or none or some of these things to the reader.

Sometime, Never was published in America in 1957 and won an accolade in the form of an Infinity Award. *Boy in Darkness* was republished in 1969 in a book called *The Inner Landscape*. In 1971 it was adapted as a short play by Paul Alexander and performed as a lunchtime play at the King's Head, Islington. In 1974 it was translated into French.

1976

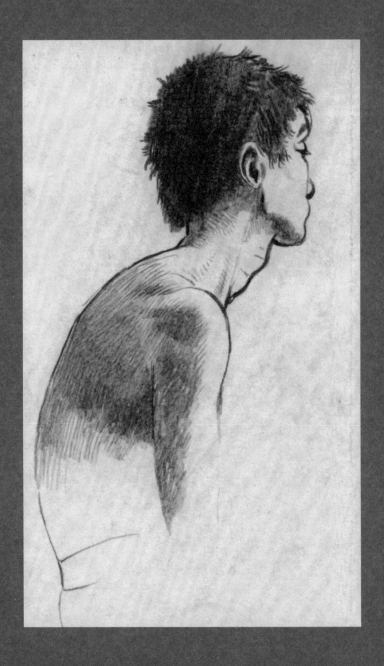

Boy in Darkness

T HE CEREMONIES WERE over for the day. The Boy was tired out. Ritual, like a senseless chariot, had rolled its wheels – and the natural life of the day was bruised and crushed.

Lord of a tower'd tract, he had no option but to be at the beck and call of those officials whose duty it was to advise and guide him. To lead him hither and thither through the mazes of his adumbrate home. To celebrate, from day to day, in remote ceremonies the meaning of which had long been forgotten.

The traditional birthday gifts had been proffered him on the tra-ditional gold tray by the Master of the Ritual. Long lines of servants, knee-deep in water, passed before him as he sat hour after hour by the margin of the gnat-haunted lake. The whole occasion had been one to try the patience of an equable adult, and for a child it was hell.

This, the Boy's birthday, was the second of the two most arduous days of the whole year. On the previous day he had been involved in a long march up the steep flanks of a hill to a plantation where it had been necessary for him to plant the fourteenth of a group of ash-trees, for today he was fourteen years old. It was no mere formality, for he had no one to help him as he worked, in a long grey cloak and a hat rather like a dunce's cap. On his return journey down the steep hill he had stumbled and fallen, bruising his knee and cutting his hand, so that, by the time he was at last alone in his small room overlooking the red-stone square, he was in a frame of mind quite savage in its resentment.

But now, on the evening of his second day, his birthday, the day of so many idiotic ceremonies that his brain throbbed with incongruous images and his body with fatigue, he lay upon his bed with his eyes closed.

After resting for some while he opened one of his eyes at what sounded like a moth fluttering against the window. He could see nothing, however, and was about to close his eyes again when he caught sight of that ochre-coloured and familiar patch of mildew that stretched across the ceiling like an island.

He had stared many times at this same mildew-island with its inlets and its bays; its coves and the long curious isthmus that joined the southern to the northern masses. He knew by heart the tapering peninsula that ended in a narrowing chain of islets like a string of discoloured beads. He knew the lakes and the rivers, and he had many a time brought imaginary ships to anchor in hazardous harbours or stood them off when the seas ran high where they rocked in his mind and set new courses for yet other lands.

But today he was too irritable to make-believe, and the only thing he stared at was a fly that was moving slowly across the island.

'An explorer, I suppose,' muttered the Boy to himself – and as he muttered there came before his eyes the hated outline of the mountain and the fourteen stupid ash-trees and the damnable presents that were handed to him on the golden tray, only to be returned to the vaults twelve hours later, and he saw a hundred familiar faces, every one of which reminded him of some ritual duty so that he beat his hands upon the bed shouting, 'No! No! No!' and sobbed until the fly on the mildew-island had crossed from east to west and was now following the coastline as though it had no wish to venture out across the ceiling-sea.

Only a little part of his consciousness was taken up with watching the fly, but that little was identifying itself with the insect so that the Boy became dimly aware of *exploration* as something more than a word or a sound of a word, as something solitary and mutinous. And then it came, all at once, the first flicker of imperative rebellion, not against any one particular person but against the eternal round of deadly symbolism.

He longed (he knew it now) to turn his anger into action – to make his escape from the gaols of precedent; to make a bid if not for final freedom then at least for a day. For a day. For one tremendous *day* of insurrection.

Insurrection! It was indeed nothing less. Was he truly contemplating so radical a step? Had he forgotten the pledges he had made as a child and on a thousand subsequent occasions? The solemn oaths that bound him, with cords of allegiance, to his home.

And then the whisper that breathed between his shoulder-blades as though urging him to fly – that whisper that was growing in volume and intensity. 'Just for a little while,' it said. 'After all you are only a boy. What kind of fun are you having?' He heaved himself over in bed and gave out a great yell.

'Oh, damn the Castle! Damn the Laws! Damn everything!' He sat bolt upright on the edge of his bed. His heart was beating fast and thick. A soft golden light was pouring through his window in a kind of haze,

and through the haze could be seen the double line of banners that shook along the roof-tops in his honour.

He took a deep breath and looked slowly around the room and was then suddenly arrested by a nearby face. It stared at him fiercely. It was a young face despite the fact that the forehead was puckered up in a deep frown. Hanging on a cord around the neck was a bunch of turkey feathers.

It was by those feathers that he knew that he was looking at himself, and he turned away from the mirror, tearing, as he did so, the absurd trophy that hung around his neck. It was for him to wear the feathers all night before handing them back on the following morning to the Hereditary Master of the Quills. As it was, he jumped from the bed, tore off the rotting relic and trampled upon it.

Then came the upsurge again! The thrill and speculation of escape.

Of escape to where? And when? *When* should it be? 'Why, now! now! now!' came the voice. 'Be up and be gone. What are you waiting for?'

But the Boy who was so fretful to be gone had another side. Something more icy, so that while his body trembled and cried his mind was not so childish. Whether to make his bid for freedom at speed and by daylight or during the long hours of darkness was not easy to decide. At first it seemed the obvious choice was to wait for the sun to sink and, taking the night for his ally, to beat his way into the fastness while the core of the castle lay heavy with sleep and smothered in ivy like a bitter veil. To creep through the labyrinthine lanes that he knew so well and out into the draughty starlit spaces and on . . . and on.

But in spite of the obvious and immediate advantages of making his escape by night yet there was the dire peril of his becoming irrevocably lost or falling into the hands of evil forces.

Fourteen years of age, he had had many opportunities to test his courage in the tortuous Castle, and he had on many an occasion been terrified, not only by the silences and glooms of the night but by a sense of being watched, almost as though the Castle itself or the spirit of the ancient place moved with him as he moved, stopped when he stopped; forever breathing at his shoulder-blades and taking note of every move he made.

Remembering these times when he had lost himself he could not but realize how much more frightening it would be for him to be alone in the darkness of a district *alien* to his life, a place remote from the kernel of the Castle where, though he detested many of the inhabitants, he was at least among his own kind. For there can be a need for hateful things and a hatred of what is, in a strange way, loved. And so a child flies to what it recognizes for recognition's sake. But to be alone in a land where nothing can be recognized, that is what he feared, and that is what he longed for. For what is exploration without peril?

But no. He would not start away in darkness. That would be madness. He would start a little before dawn with most of the Castle asleep,

and he would run through the half-light and race the sun – he on the ground and the sun in the air – the two of them, alone.

But how to bear the cold, slow-footed night – the interminable night that lay ahead? Sleep seemed impossible, though sleep he needed. He slid off his bed and walked rapidly to the window. The sun was not far above the notched horizon, and all things swam in a pale translucency. But not for long. The gentle vista took, all of a sudden, another aspect. Towers that a moment ago had been ethereal, and all but floated in the golden air, had now become, through loss of the sun's late beams, like black and carious teeth.

A shudder ran over the darkened terrain, and the first of the night-owls floated noiselessly past the window. Far below him a voice was shouting. It was too far away for the words to be decipherable but not too far for them to be coloured with anger. Another voice took up the argument. Titus leant over the window-sill and stared down vertically. The antagonists were the size of sunflower seeds. A bell began to chime, and then another and then a swarm of bells. Harsh bells and mellow ones; bells of many metals and many ages; bells of fear and bells of anger; gay bells and mournful; thick bells and clear bells . . . the flat and the resonant, the exultant and the sad. For a few moments they filled the air together; a murmuration; with a clamour of tongues that spread their echoes over the great shell of the Castle like a shawl of metal. Then one by one the tumult weakened and scores of bells fell away until there was nothing but an uneasy silence, until, infinitely far away, a slow and husky voice stumbled its way over the roof-tops and the Boy at the window heard the last of the thick notes die into silence.

For a moment he was caught up in the familiar splendour of it all. He never tired of the bells. Then just as he was about to turn from the window there came another peal of such urgency as to make him frown, for he could not think what it could mean. Then came another peal and then another, and after the fourteenth had ended it was clear that he was being saluted. He had forgotten for a little while his status, only to be reminded with a jolt. He could not escape his birthright. It might be thought to have such deference shown him could not but give pleasure to a boy. But it was not so in the case of the young earl. His whole life had been swamped with ceremony, and his happiest moments were when he was alone.

Alone. Alone? That meant *away*. Away, but where? That lay beyond his powers to imagine.

Beyond the window the night was heavy with its own darkness, only interrupted by the pinpoints of light that flickered along the backbone of that same steep-sided mountain he had climbed and in whose flank he had planted the fourteenth ash-tree. These distant sparks or embers burnt not only on the mountain but along the periphery of a great circle – and it was in obedience to the beckoning bonfires that crowds were beginning to form in a score of courtyards.

For tonight was the night of high barbecue, and within a little while long lines of retainers would be on their way to one or other section of the circle. The Castle would empty itself, and men on horseback, men on foot, mules and carriages and all sorts of vehicles would set out. And, leaping to and fro in anticipation, a crowd of urchins would scream and fight, their cries like the cries of starlings.

It was these cries that now rose through the dark air that upset whatever plans he had formed and whatever wisdom the Boy possessed. They were shrill with the excitement of childhood, and standing at the window he suddenly and without conscious thought knew positively, knew absolutely, that he must escape now: now in the thick and turmoil of it all. Now, while ritual rang with bells and bonfires: now, on the crest of decision.

He was agile, and he needed to be, for the course he set for himself was hazardous. This was no mere matter of rushing down long flights of stairs. This was at once something faster and more secretive.

For many years he had, out of sheer inquisitiveness, pried here and there among the dust-filled rooms of his seemingly endless home until he had discovered a dozen ways of reaching the ground without touching the main stairways and without being seen. If there was ever a time for him to use his knowledge this was it, so at the T-shaped ending of the forty-foot corridor along which he was racing he turned neither right to the northern, nor left to the southern stairs that swept down, down, down, in scything curves of worm-riddled wood, but instead he jumped for a small glassless window immediately overhead, and, catching hold of a short stub-end of rope that protruded from the window-base, he hauled himself up and through . . .

Stretching before him was a long attic, the beams of which were so low that to make progress there was no question of merely stooping, let alone walking upright. The only method was to lie flat and wriggle on knees and elbows. This could be a wearisome business, for the attic was extensive, but the Boy had reduced the process to such a rhythmic science that to see him would be like watching a mechanical toy.

At the far end there was a trapdoor which, when pulled open on its hinge, disclosed, from above, a long drop to an outstretched blanket like a huge blue hammock. The corners were tied with cord attached to the low beams; the belly of the blanket swung free of the ground.

Within a few moments he was through the trapdoor and had bounced from the blanket on to the floor like an acrobat. This room must once have been cared for. There were signs of faded elegance, but the high, square room now breathed a forlorn and dismal air.

Had it not been that the window of this room was thrown wide to the night, the Boy might by now have been finding it impossible to see his hand before his face. But the window made a rectangle of dark grey that appeared to be let in to surrounding blackness of the room.

Moving rapidly to the window, he edged his way over the sill and out into the open air and now began the long swarm down a hundred feet of tough grey rope.

After what seemed to be a long while he reached another small window in the enormous expanse of the wall, and he wriggled his way through this disused opening and left the long rope swinging aimlessly.

Now he was on some kind of a landing, and a moment later he was pounding his way down flight after flight of stairs until he came to a derelict hall.

At the Boy's approach a husky scuffling sound suggested that a number of little creatures had been startled and were making for their lairs.

The floor of the one-time hall was not a floor in the ordinary sense, for the floorboards had long since rotted away, and where they should have been the grass grew luxuriantly and a host of molehills filled the place as though it were an ancient burial ground.

For a few moments, not knowing why, he stood still and listened. It was not the kind of place for racing through, for there is a certain grandeur in decay and in stillness, which slows the footsteps.

When he halted there was no sound at all, but now, as from another world, he heard the far-away voices of children, so faint that at first he thought it was the sound of a beetle rubbing its thighs together.

He turned to his left where there was once the door, and at the far end of a corridor he saw the small square of light no bigger than a fingernail. He began to make his way down this corridor, but there was a different air about him now. The madness had gone out of his flight. He was moving gingerly.

For there was a light at the far end of the corridor. A dull red glow suggesting sundown. What could it be? The sun had sunk long ago.

Then came far, shrill voices again, this time louder, though no single word could be recognized: and then he realized what was happening.

The children of the Castle were at large. It was their night of nights with torches blazing. Their voices grew louder as the Boy advanced, until he saw them through the archway and they covered the ground, an army of wild children, so that he found no difficulty in slipping unobserved into their teeming ranks. The torches flared in the voice-filled night, and the light of the torches shone on their wet foreheads and flashed in their eyes. And the Boy marched with them until, realizing that they were making for the traditional Torch Mountain, he gradually dropped behind and, choosing his moment, he sheered off at a junction where the trees grew thickly among high mounds of masonry and he was, once again, alone.

By now he was several miles from the Castle itself and deep into less obvious territory; less obvious but still recognizable by reason of the occasional idiosyncrasy of stone or metal. A shape protruding from a wall, a jag or jutting that rose to the brink of memory.

So the Boy moved on and on, catching glimpse after glimpse of half-remembered, half-forgotten shapes; but these shapes that clung to his mind because of their peculiarities (a stain across the ground the shape of a three-fingered hand or the spiral movement of a branch above his head) became, as he proceeded, further and further apart, and the time came when, for a quarter of an hour, he was alone with no mark or sign to guide him.

It was as though he had been deserted by the outriders of his memory, and an uprush of fear flowed over him like an icy wave.

He turned in the darkness, this way and that, flashing his torch along the endless walk to set the webs of spiders in a blaze or blind a lizard on its ferny shelf. There was no one about, and the only sound was the slow drip of water and the occasional rustling of ivy.

Then he remembered his motive, his reason for being where he was: lost in a fastness; he remembered the endless ritual of his primordial home; he remembered his anger and how he was determined to defy the sacred laws of his family and his kingdom; and he stamped his feet on the ground. For, in spite of all this, he was frightened at what he had done and frightened of the night, and he began to run, his footsteps sounding loud upon the stones, until he came to a great stretch of land where only a few trees grew with their arms flung out as though in exasperation, and as he ran the moon slid out of the thick clouds and he saw ahead of him a river.

A river! What river could this be? There was, it is true, a river that wound about his home, but this was something quite different – a wide, sluggish waterway with no trees upon its banks, a featureless, slow-moving stretch of sullen water with the bilious moonlight glowering on its back.

He had come to a halt on seeing this, and as he stood he felt the darkness close in behind him so that he turned his head and saw the dogs.

Out of nowhere, it seemed, these hounds had gathered themselves together. Never in his life had the Boy seen so many. There had been, of course, the scavengers, flitting from time to time down the corridors of his home, hugging the walls, baring their fangs – the shadow, the yelp and a scuffle in the dark – and then the silence again. But this was something very different, where the dogs seemed to be a part of the day and night, cocksure of themselves, their lean grey heads held high in the air. Hounds out of somewhere else – they lived in forsaken halls and lay down all together in a single blot of darkness – or in the glaring noon they covered the stone floors of ruined cloisters as thick on the ground as autumn leaves.

They gathered themselves in a half-moon and, without touching him, seemed yet to *urge* him eastwards to the bank of the great river.

The breath from their lungs was deep and fierce, but there seemed to

be no immediate menace in it. Not by the merest graze did the fanged horde of these hounds touch the Boy, who was yet impelled to go forward inch by inch until he stood on the brink of the great waterway where a shallow skiff lay moored. With the breathing of the beasts all about him he stepped down into the skiff and, with shaking hands, untied the painter. Then grabbing a kind of punting pole he pushed off into the sluggish stream. But he was not free of the dogs who, leaping into the water, surrounded him so that a great flotilla of canine heads bobbed up and down in the moon-glazed water, their ears pointed, their fangs bright in the light of the moon. But it was their eyes that were appalling, for they were that kind of bright and acid yellow that allowed no other colour alongside and, if a colour can have any moral value, was ineradicably wicked.

Fearful as he was, and amazed as he was to find himself in this strange predicament, yet, in spite of the pack, he was less ill with terror than he might have been utterly alone. The dogs were, unwittingly, his companions. They, unlike the iron and the stone, were alive and had in common with him the throb of life in their breasts, and he threw up a prayer of gladness as he dug the long pole into the mud of the riverbed.

But he was deadly tired, and his weariness joined with the easing of his loneliness to the point where he all but fell asleep. But he kept his eyelids open and the time came when he reached the opposite bank and stepped out over the side into the warm moonlit water and the hounds turned about and drifted away like a dark carpet.

So he was alone again, and his terror might have returned had he not been so tired. As it was, he crawled up a shallow bank until he reached dry ground and then, curling up, he fell incontinently asleep.

How long he slept was difficult for him to estimate, but when he woke it was broad daylight, and as he raised himself on one arm he knew that all was ill. This was not the air of his own country. This was foreign air. He looked about and nothing was familiar. He had known on the previous night that he was lost, but this was another kind of sensation, for it seemed that he was not only far from home but that some new quality hovered between him and the sun. It was not that something had gone that in his heart of hearts he wanted back but that something lay ahead of him that he had no wish to meet. What it could be he had no inkling. All he knew was that it would be different. The sun upon his face felt hot and very dry. His sight appeared to be keener than ever, as though a film had been taken away from his eyes, and an odour quite unlike any other began to force itself upon his notice.

It was not unpleasant in itself. In fact there was a trace of sweetness inextricably tangled with the menace.

He turned his back upon the wide and creeping river and, leaving the skiff in the shallow water, clenched his hands together. Then he started to walk with quick, nervous steps towards the low hills that lay over the skyline where walls and roof-tops were intermixed with trees and the branches of trees.

As he went on there were indications, at first hardly recognizable, that he was on evil ground. Tinges of glaucous colour, now here, now there, appeared before his eyes. They lay thinly like snail-slime or glistened from the occasional stone or along a blade of grass or spread like a blush over the ground.

But a blush that was grey. A wet and slippery thing that moved hither and thither over the foreign ground. It shone with a horrible light upon the dark earth – and then was gone and the reverse took its place, for the blush was now the dark and slithering thing and the terrain all about it shone like the skin of a leper.

The Boy turned his head from something he could not understand in order to rest his eyes upon – the river, for even that ghastly waterway was some kind of a comfort, for it was in the past and the past can do no further harm. It had done him none. As for the dogs, not one had harmed him, though the panting of their lungs was frightful. It was their eyes that had been devilish.

There was no such colour now that the daylight had returned. The sun, for all its strength, gave out the kind of light that sucked out every hue. For the moon to have done this would have been in keeping with the baleful light she casts, but in her case something of the reverse had happened, for the eyes were lemon-yellow.

But when the Boy turned to the waterway behind him, as though for comfort, he saw how changed it was. Whatever it had been like on that previous night, it was no friend to him now. The water under the sun's rays was like grey oil that heaved as though with a voluptuous sickness. The Boy turned his head back again and ran a little way as though from some vile beast.

In contrast to the oleaginous river the harsh outline of the wooded hill was crusty like bread, and with never a glance behind him he made in that direction.

It was now many hours since he had last had a meal, and his hunger was becoming almost unbearable. The level ground was thick with dust.

Perhaps it was this soft white dust that killed the sound of approaching footsteps: for the Boy had no suspicion that something was approaching him. It was not until a waft of sour breath touched him that he started and leapt to one side and faced the newcomer.

The face was unlike anything the boy had ever seen before. It was too big. Too long. Too shaggy. Too massive altogether for decency, for there is a kind of malproportion that is best kept away from public view.

The figure who stood so upright (even to the extent of appearing to lean backward a little as though recoiling) was dressed in a dark and ridiculously voluminous suit of some thick material. The starched cuffs, which had once been white, were so long and loose that they completely covered up his hands.

He wore no hat, but a mass of dusty little curls covered his cranium and spread down the back of his neck.

The protruding and osseous temples appeared to be thrusting their way through the wig-like hair. The eyes were horribly paled and glassy, with such small pupils as to be virtually invisible.

If the Boy was not able to take in everything at a glance, he was at least able to know that he was facing something that could never have been discovered in the precincts of his home. It was in some way of another order. And yet what was it that made this gentleman so different? His hair was curly and dusty. This was somehow revolting, but there was nothing *monstrous* about it. The head was long and huge. But why should that, in itself, be repellent or impossible? The eyes were pale, and almost pupil-less, but what of that? The pupil was there, though tiny, and there was obviously no need for its enlargement.

The Boy dropped his eyes for the merest fraction of a second, for one of the feet had raised itself into the air and was scratching the thigh of the opposite leg with horrid deliberation.

The Boy shuddered a little, but why? The gentleman had done nothing wrong.

Yet all was different. All was wrong, and the Boy, whose heart was beating thick and fast, watched the newcomer with apprehension. It was then that the long hirsute head lowered itself and rolled a little from side to side.

'What do you want?' said the Boy. 'Who are you?'

The gentleman ceased to swing his head about and looked fixedly at the Boy, baring his teeth in a smile.

'Who are you?' the Boy repeated. 'What is your name?'

The black-coated figure leant back in his tracks, so that there was something pompous about him. But the smile was still spread across his face like a dazzling wound.

'I am Goat,' he said, and the noise of it came thickly from between his shining teeth. 'I have come to welcome you, child. Yes . . . yes . . . to welcome you . . .'

The man who called himself Goat then took a sidelong step towards the Boy – a vile and furtive step which, when it had reached its limit of extension, began to oscillate a hoof-like shoe that, as it dropped the white dust to and fro in an almost prudish way, revealed a central crack along the welt. The boy retreated involuntarily but could not help staring at the beastly terminal as he did so. This cracked foot was not of a kind of thing that any right-minded man would care to exhibit to a stranger. But the Goat did nothing but shift it to and fro, only ceasing from time to time to watch the soft sand as it poured back from the split and on to the ground again.

'Child,' he said (still scraping the sand about), 'wince not away from me. Shall I carry you?'

'No!' cried the Boy, in so quick and loud a voice that the smile of the Goat went off and on again like a light.

'Very well,' said the Goat, 'then you must walk.'

'Where to?' said the Boy. 'I think I would like to go home.'

'That is just where you *are* going, child,' said the Goat, and then in a kind of ruminative afterthought he repeated the words. 'That is just where you are going.'

'To the Castle?' said the Boy. 'To my room? Where I can rest?'

'Oh, no, not there,' said the Goat. 'Nothing to do with any *castle*.'

'Where I can rest,' repeated the Boy, 'and have something to eat. I am very hungry', and then a fit of temper ran through him and he shouted at the black-suited, long-headed Goat, 'Hungry! Hungry!' and he stamped his foot on the ground.

'There will be a banquet for you,' said the Goat. 'It will be held in the Iron Room. You are the first.'

'The first what?' said the Boy.

'The first visitor. You are what we have been waiting for so long. Would you like to stroke my beard?'

'No,' said Titus. 'Get away from me.'

'Now that's a cruel thing to say to me,' said the Goat, 'especially as

I'm the kindest one of all. You wait till you see the others. You are just what they want.'

Then the Goat began to laugh, and his large, loose white cuffs flipped to and fro as he beat his arms at his sides.

'I tell you what,' it said. 'If you tell me things, then I'll tell you things. How would you like that?' The Goat leant forward and gazed at the Boy with his empty-looking eyes.

'I don't know what you mean,' whispered the Boy, 'but find me food or I will never do anything for you, I will hate you even more – and I will kill you – yes, kill you because of my hunger. Get me bread! Get me bread!'

'Bread is not good enough for you,' said the Goat. 'Oh dear, no. What you need are things like figs and rushes.' He bent over the Boy, and his black greasy coat smelt faintly of ammonia. 'And another thing you need is . . .'

He did not finish his sentence because the boy gave at the knees and slumped to the ground in a dead faint.

The long hairy jaws of the Goat fell open like those of a mechanical toy, and dropping to his knees he shook his head in an inane way, so that the dry dust that covered the curls on his head rose and drifted away in the joyless sunlight. When the Goat had stared for some time he rose to his feet and sidled away for perhaps twenty or thirty paces, looking over his shoulder every so often to make sure that he was not mistaken. But no. There was the Boy where he left him, motionless as ever. Then the Goat turned in his tracks and gazed at the rough horizon where trees and hills were knotted together in a long string. And as he watched he saw, a long way off, something no larger than an insect running. It seemed at times to be on all fours but then to change to run almost upright, and the effect upon the Goat was immediate.

A gleam of dull light that had both fear and vengeance in it flickered for a moment across the blank of the Goat's eyes, and he began to paw the ground, sending up spurts of white gravelly dust. Then he returned at a trot to the Boy, and, lifting him with an ease that suggested that a terrible strength lay hidden within the loose ammonia-smelling jacket, he slung him like a sack over his shoulder and then began to make for the horizon with a kind of awkward sideways run.

And as he ran on and on over the white dust he muttered to himself. 'First of all our sovereign lord of the white head, the Lamb, and there is only the Lamb, for he is the heart of life and love, and that is true because he *tells* us so. So first of all I call to him through darkness. To be received. And I will be rewarded, it may be, by the soft vice in his voice. And that is true because he told me so. And it is very secret and Hyena must not know . . . Hyena must not know . . . because I found him on my very own. So Hyena must not see me or the creature . . . the hungry creature . . . the creature we have waited for so long . . . My present to the Lamb . . . the Lamb, his master . . . lord of the snow-white . . . the very Lamb.'

As he ran, in that sideways manner, he continued to pour out the thoughts as they bubbled up confusedly at the brink of his poor deluded brain. His power of running seemed to have no bounds. He did not pant or gasp for air. Only once did he stop and that was in order to scratch his head deep down in the undergrowth of his dusty, verminous curls where his forehead and his crown were itching as though his head was on fire. To do this he had to place the Boy on the ground, and it was at about this point that a few grass-blades could be seen pushing up through the dust. The wooded hills were by now appreciably closer, and, as the Goat scratched his head and while this operation was sending up clouds of dust that hung in the air, the creature who had been observed in the distance once again made its appearance.

But the Goat had his head turned away from that direction, and it was the Hyena who, loping back from some wickedness or other, suddenly saw his colleague and froze on the instant where he stood, like a thing of metal, its animal ears pricked forward sharply. Its protruding

eyes were filled with the Goat and with something else. What was that shape that lay on the dust at the Goat's feet?

For some while he could not make it out, even with his acute and comprehensive eyesight – but then, as the Goat turned to the Boy, shaking down his long cuffs still further as he did so, and, as he picked the Boy up with his forearm and slung him over his back, Hyena could see the outline of a human face, and as he saw this he began to tremble with so terrible a vitality of the blood that the distant Goat stared about him as though there was a change in the weather or as though the sky had changed colour.

Feeling the change but not knowing what to do about it, for nothing was to be seen or heard, the Goat began to run again, his black cloak-like coat flapping out behind him and the Boy over his shoulder.

Hyena watched carefully, for the Goat was by now within a few hundred yards of the periphery of the wooded hills. Once in the shadow of the trees it was not easy to track down a foe or find a friend.

But Hyena, though noting with care the direction of the Goat's progress, was nevertheless pretty sure of his route and his destination. For, as Hyena knew, the Goat was a lickspittle and a toady, who would never dare to risk the wrath of the Lamb. That is where he would be going. To the heart of the terrain where deep in the silence stood the Warehouses.

So the Hyena waited a little while, and, as he watched, the air around him was loud with the sound of bones being cracked, for Hyena was fond of marrow and kept a quiverful of bones in his pocket. His jaws were very powerful, and as he crunched the muscles could be seen working between his ears and his jaw; and this was made all the more apparent by the fact that Hyena, in contrast to the Goat, was something of a dandy, shaving himself with a cut-throat razor with great care every five or six hours. For the bristles on his jowl were tough and rapid and had to be dealt with. His long forearms were another matter. Thickly covered with a brindled growth, they were something to be proud of, and for this reason Hyena was never to be seen in a jacket. The shirt he wore was cut off very short in the sleeves so that his long spotted arms could be readily appreciated. But by far the most impressive thing about him was his mane that billowed down through a vent in the shirt between the shoulder-blades. His trousered legs were very narrow and very short, so that his back, as a result, was at a very steep incline. So much so, in fact, that he was often to be seen dropping his long-armed forelegs to the ground.

There was about him something very foul. As with the Goat it was difficult to pin this foulness down to any particular feature, horrid enough as that may have been. But there was a kind of menace all the same about Hyena; a menace very different from the vague beastliness of the Goat. Less unctuous, less stupid, less dirty than the Goat, but bloodier, crueller and with a fiercer blood-drive, and for all the ease with which the Goat had shouldered the Boy a bestial strength of quite a different order. That clean white shirt, wide open at the front, disclosed a hinterland, black and rocklike.

Bobbing about in the half-darkness was a blood-ruby that hung and smouldered on a big golden chain.

There he stood, at midday, at the edge of the wood, his eyes fixed upon Goat with the Boy on his shoulders. And as he stood there he cocked his head on one side and at the same time brought out of his trousers pocket a great knuckle of bone the size of a doorknob, and, nuzzling this seemingly intractable thing between his eye-teeth, he cracked it open as though it were an egg-shell.

Then he drew on a pair of yellow gloves (his eyes never leaving the Goat), and, unhooking his walking-cane from the branch of a nearby tree, he suddenly turned and dived into the shadows of the forest trees that stood motionless like some kind of ominous curtain.

Once among the trees and the little hills he tucked the cane, for safe keeping, through the hairs of his shaggy mane and, dropping his forelegs to the ground, began to gallop through the semi-darkness as though he were an animal. And as he ran he began to laugh, mournfully at first, until this unhappy sound gave place by degrees to another kind of beast-liness. There is a kind of laughter that sickens the soul. Laughter when it is out of control: when it screams and stamps its feet, and sets the bells jangling in the next town. Laughter in all its ignorance and its cruelty. Laughter with the seed of Satan in it. It tramples upon shrines; the belly-roarer. It roars, it yells, it is delirious: and yet it is as cold as ice. It has no humour. It is naked noise and naked malice, and such was Hyena's.

For Hyena had such raw vitality of the blood, such brutal ebul-lience, that as he ran over the ferns and grasses a kind of throbbing went with him. An almost audible thing, in the profound silence of the forest. For there was a sense of silence in spite of the monstrous and idiotic laughter, a silence more deadly than any long-drawn stillness, for every fresh burst was like a knife wound, every silence a new nullity.

But by degrees the laughter grew less and less, until he came to a clearing among the trees and there was no noise at all. He had travelled very fast and was not surprised to find that he had outstripped the Goat, for he was confident, nor was he wrong, that the Goat would be making for the mines. Certain that he would not have long to wait, Hyena sat upright on a boulder and began to readjust his clothes, darting a glance from time to time at a gap in the trees.

As nothing appeared for some while, Hyena began to study his long, powerful and brindled forearms and seemed pleased with what he saw, for groups of muscles moved across his shaven cheeks and the corner of his mouth lifted into what might have been either a smile or a snarl, and a moment later there was a sound of something moving among the branches, and there, all at once, was the Goat.

The Boy, still in a faint, hung limply over the black-clothed shoulder. For some while the Goat stood quite still, not because he had seen Hyena but because this glade, or clearing, was like a stage or a land-mark in his progress, and he paused, involuntarily, to rest. The sunlight fell upon his knobbly forehead. The long, dirty white cuffs swung to and fro, annihilating whatever hands he possessed. His long jacket, so black in the semi-darkness, had about it, in the sunlight, a greenish tinge that suggested decay.

Hyena, who had been sitting motionless on his boulder, now got to his feet, and a bestial strength was redolent in every movement he made. But the Goat had begun to shift the Boy on to his other shoulder and Hyena was still unobserved, until a crack like a rifle-shot caused the Goat to wheel about on his cracked shoes and at the same moment to drop his precious burden.

It was a sound he recognized, that whip-crack, that gunshot, for it was, along with the cracking and crunching, as much a part of Hyena's existence as the mane on the back of his spotted forearms.

'Fool of a fool!' cried Hyena. 'Clot! Lout! And damnable Goat! Come here before I add another bump to your dirty brow! And bring that bundle with you,' he said, pointing at the heap on the forest floor. He did not know any more than the Goat that the Boy was watching them through half-closed eyes.

The Goat did a sideways shuffle and then displayed his teeth in the most fatuous of dazzling smiles.

'Hyena, dear,' he said. 'How well you are looking! Quite your own self again, I shouldn't wonder. Bless your long forearms and your splendid mane.'

'Forget my forearms, Goat! Fetch me the bundle.'

'And so I will,' said the Goat. 'Indeed and of course.' And the Goat drew the swathes of his filthy jacket about him as though he were cold and sidled away to where the Boy lay seemingly inert.

'Is he dead?' said Hyena. 'If so, I'll crack your leg-bone. He must be living when we take him there.'

'*We* take him there? Is that what you said?' said the Goat. 'By the splendour of your mane, Hyena, dear, you are despising me. It is *I* who, found him. *I*, Capricorn, the Goat . . . if you'll forgive me. I shall take him alone.'

Then the vile blood leapt in the veins of the brute. With one great spring, the sinewy Hyena was upon the Goat and was holding him down. The surge of sheer, malicious, uncontrollable vitality shook his frame as though to shake it to pieces, so that while Hyena held the Goat helpless on its back (for his hands gripped the poor creature by its shoulders) he trod savagely to and fro along the length of his victim, his cruel hands remaining where they were.

The Boy lay quietly watching the brutal scene. His soul retched as he watched, and it was all he could do to stop himself getting to his feet and running. But he knew that he had no chance against the two of them. Even were he to have been strong and well, he could never have escaped from the bounding Hyena, whose body appeared to contain the spleen and energy of Satan himself.

As it was, lying alone on the wide floor of a foreign world, his limbs as heavy as lead, the very idea of escape was ludicrous.

But he had not let the moments go by without some reward. He had learnt from broken sentences that there was Another. Another creature – a creature vague and tenuous in the Boy's mind but something that assumed some kind of power, not only over the Goat but the impetuous Hyena also – and perhaps over others.

The Goat, muscular as he was, gave in entirely to Hyena, for he knew the brindled beast of old and to what cruelties he could resort were he to have put up any resistance. As it was, the Hyena sprang away from the bruised Goat and rearranged the folds of his white shirt. The eyes in his long, lean face shone with a disgusting light.

'Has your foul carcass had enough of it? Eh? Why he puts up with you is beyond me.'

'Because he's blind,' whispered the Goat. 'You ought to know *that*, Hyena, dear. Ah me, how rough you are.'

'Rough? That was nothing! Why –'

'No, no, my dear. There's no need to tell me. I know you are stronger than I am. So there is little I can do.'

'There's nothing you can do,' said Hyena. 'Repeat it after me.'

'What?' said the Goat, who was by now sitting up. 'I don't quite understand you, Hyena, my love.'

'If you call me your love again, I'll skin you,' said Hyena, and he brought out a long, slim blade. The sunbeams danced upon it.

'Yes . . . yes . . . I've seen it before,' said the Goat. 'I know all about that sort of thing. After all, you have bullied me for years and years, haven't you?' and he flashed his fatuous smile so that his teeth looked like a graveyard. Never was there a mouth so empty of mirth. He turned from the Hyena and made his way again to where the Boy lay silently, but, before he reached the seemingly insensate bundle, he turned and cried: 'Oh, but it's shameful. It was I who found him – found him alone in the white dust, and it was I who crept up to him and surprised him. It was all my doing, and now I must share it. Oh, Hyena! Hyena! You are more brutal than I, and you must have your way.'

'And so I shall. Never fear,' said the Hyena, cracking a fresh bone between his teeth and spitting out a cloud of white powder.

'But, oh, it's the glory that I need,' said the Goat. 'It's the glory of it.'

'Ah,' said Hyena. 'You are lucky that I let you come at all – you knobhead.'

At this pleasantry the Goat merely scratched himself, but with such force that the dust arose from every corner of his anatomy so that he was for a few moments quite invisible in a small column of white dust. Then he turned his baleful, all-but-pupil-less pale eyes upon his companion, and then with his inimitable sideways trot he approached the Boy – but before he had reached him Hyena came hurtling through the air and was already sitting very upright by the Boy's side.

'You see my mane, don't you, cockroach?'

'Of course I do,' said the Goat. 'It needs oiling!'

'Silence!' said Hyena. 'Do what I tell you!'

'What would that be, Hyena, dear?'

'Plait my mane!'

'Oh, no!' cried Goat. 'Not now . . .'

'Plait my mane!'

'What then, Hyena?'

'Plait the six ropes of it!'

'What for, my dear?'

'For to tie him to me with. I shall take him on my back to the Lamb. That will please the Lamb. So plait my mane and bind him to the plaits. Then I can run, you shuffling sod! Run as only I can run. I can run like the wind I can, like the black winds from the wastelands. I am the fastest in the world. Faster than my fastest foe. As for my strength – the very finest lions vomit and slink away. Who else has arms like mine. Even the very Lamb admired them long ago . . . in the days when he could see me. Oh, fool of a fool! you sicken me. Plait my mane. My black mane! What are you waiting for?'

'I found him in the dust-lands by myself, and now you . . .'

But the Goat was interrupted by a movement in the tail of his eye and, turning his dusty head quickly in the direction of the Boy, he saw him get to his feet. At the same moment Hyena ceased in his crunching of a marrowy knuckle, and for a few moments the three of them stood quite still. Around them the leaves of the trees fluttered but made no sound. There were no birds. There was nothing, it seemed, that was alive. The ground itself had a deadness about it. No insects made their way from grass blade to grass blade or from stone to stone. The sun shone down in a dead, flat heat.

The Boy, who, weak as he was, and frightened as he was, had nevertheless been listening to the conversation, and he had gathered one or two thoughts together, and it was he who broke the stillness with his young voice.

'In the name of the Blind Lamb,' he cried, 'salutations to you both.' He turned to Hyena. 'May the spots upon your magnificent forearms never grow faint with the lashing of the winter rains or black in the summer sun.'

He paused. His heart was beating violently. His taut limbs trembled. But he felt the silence of their concentration grow; so intently did they stare at him.

He knew he must go on.

'And what a mane! How proud and arrogant are the hairs of it! With what a black, torrential surge do they break through your snow-white shirt. Let it never be rearranged or altered in any way, this wrath of a mane, save to be combed by moonlight when the owls are hunting. Oh, splendid creature. And what a jaw for cracking. Indeed you must be proud of the power in your tendons and the granite of your teeth.'

The Boy turned his head to the Goat and drew in a deep shuddering breath. 'Ah, Goat,' he said. 'We have met before. I remember you so well. Was it in this world or the last? I remember the amplitude of your smile and the serene detachment of your gaze. But, oh, what was it about your walk? What was it? There was something that was so very personal about it. Would you walk for me, Mr Goat? Out of the kindness of your heart. Would you walk so far as that tree and back? Will you? So that I can remember?'

For a moment or two there was no sound. It seemed that Goat and Hyena were rooted where they stood. They had never heard such eloquence. They had never been so amazed. The bundle of weakness over whose prostrate body they had been arguing was now standing between them.

Then the air became suddenly mournful as a far-away howl was heard, but only for a moment, for it then turned into a scream of penetrating laughter – mirthless, hideous. The whole vast, muscular body shook and shook as though to shake the life out of itself. The head of the Hyena was thrown back, its throat taut with the passion of its outcry. Then all was over. The fierce head sunk to the level of the huge white-shirted shoulders.

The head of the Hyena turned not to the Boy but to the Goat.

'Do as you're told,' he cried. 'Insolent dust-bag, clod and filthy knobhead. Do what you're told before I crunch your skull.' Hyena turned to the Boy. 'He's as dense as a nag's heel. Look at him now.'

'Which tree do you mean?' said Goat, scratching himself.

'The nearest tree, Mr Goat. How is it that you walk? I can't remember. Ah, that's it, that's it! Sideways like a ship in a beam sea. Sideways and edgeways with your cargo slipping. Ah, Mr Goat, it is strange and haunting, the way you proceed across the face of the earth. Certainly you are a pair of originals, and as such I hail you in the name of Blind Lamb.'

'The Blind Lamb,' repeated the pair. 'Hail to the Blind Lamb.'

'And also, in his name,' said the Boy, 'have mercy on my hunger. That you had thought of your mane as my cradle showed great original- ity – but I would die of proximity. The working of your muscles would be too much for me. The splendid rankness of your mane would be too strong. The throbbing of your heart would batter me. I have no strength for that. You are so tremendous . . . so majestic. Make me, out of your ingenuity a chair of branches, and carry me both of you . . . carry me . . . where . . . Oh, where will you carry me to?'

'Branches! Branches!' yelled Hyena, taking no notice of the ques- tion. 'What are you waiting for?' and he gave the Goat a great swipe and then proceeded to break branches off the nearby trees and to thread them together. The tearing of the branches from the main limbs of the trees sounded both loud and terrible in the still air. The Boy sat still, watching these two sinister creatures at work in the shadow of the trees, and he wondered how and where he could escape from their vile presence. It was obvious that to escape from them now would lead him to starvation. To whoever it was that they were determined to take him, they would surely have at least bread to eat and water to drink.

The Hyena was on his way back from the trees. He had dropped the saddle-like chair which he had been making and was, it seemed, in

a great hurry to reach the Boy. When he arrived he seemed unable to express himself and, though his jaws worked spasmodically, no words ventured forth from his unpleasant mouth. At last in a brutal rush –

'You!' he shouted. 'What do you know of the Lamb? The secret Lamb! The Lamb, our Emperor. How dare you talk of the Lamb . . . the Blind Lamb for whom we exist. We are all that is left of them . . . of all the creatures of the globe; of all insects and all birds – of the fish of the salt ocean and the beasts of prey. For he has changed their natures, and they have died. But we did not die. We became as we are through the powers of the Lamb and from his terrible skill. How have you heard of him, you from the white-dust region? Look! You are no more than a youth. How have you heard of him?'

'Oh, I am but a figment of his thought,' said the Boy. 'I am not really here. Not in my own right. I am here because he made me. But I have wandered – wandered away from his great brain. He does not wish to own me any more. Take me to somewhere where I can eat and drink, then let me go again.'

Meanwhile the Goat had reappeared.

'He is hungry,' said the Goat, but as he said it the vapid smile on his face froze into something that spelt terror, for from far away there came a sound – a sound that appeared to proceed from unimaginable depths. It was a thin sound, clear as the tinkling of an icicle. Faint, far and clear.

The effect upon the Hyena was as instantaneous as it was upon the Goat. His pointed ears were all at once pricked forward. His head lifted itself high into the air – and the colour of the jowl, which he so carefully shaved each morning, changed from a mottled purple to a deathly pallor.

The Boy, who had heard the call no less than the others, could not imagine why such a sweet and liquid sound should have such an effect upon the two rigid creatures at his side.

'What was that?' he said at last. 'Why are you so frightened?'

After a long silence they answered him together.

'That was our Master *bleating*.'

Far away beyond the power of search, in the breathless wastes, where time slides on and on through the sickness of day and the suffocation of the night, there was a land of absolute stillness – a stillness of breath indrawn and held in the lungs – the stillness of apprehension and a dire suspense.

And at the heart of this land or region, where no trees grew, and no birds sang, there was a desert of grey space that shone with a metallic light.

Dropping imperceptibly from the four horizons this wide swathe of terrain, as if drawn in towards a centre, began, hardly noticeably at first, to break into terraces bright and lifeless, and, as the level of the surrounding land subsided, the terraces grew steeper and wider until, just when it appeared that the focus of this wilderness was at hand, the grey terraces ceased and there was spread out to the gaze a field of naked stone. Scattered indiscriminately across this field was what looked like the chimneys or shafts of old metal workings, mine-heads, and littered here and there in every direction girders and chains. And over it all the light shone horribly on metal and stone.

And while the mocking sun poured out its beams, and while there was no other movement in the whole vast amphitheatre, there was something stirring, something far below the level of the ground. Something that was alone and alive, something that smiled very gently to itself as it sat upon a throne in a great vaulted chamber, lit by a crowd of candles.

But for all the effulgence thrown out by these candles, the greater part of the vault was thick with shadow. The contrast between the dead and glowing light of the outer world with its hot, metallic sheen, and the chiaroscuro of this subterranean vault, was something that the Goat and the Hyena, insensitive as they were, never failed to be aware of.

Nor, though the sense of beauty was painfully absent from their natures, were they ever able to enter this particular chamber without wonder and stupefaction. Living  and sleeping, as they did, in dark and filthy cells, for they were not allowed so much as a single candle, Hyena and the Goat had once upon a time been rebellious. They had seen no reason why, because they were not so intelligent as their overlord, they should have been worse served in the comforts of life. But that was very long ago, and they had now known for many years that they were of a lesser breed and that to serve and obey their master was its own reward. Besides, how would they survive without his brains? Was it not worth all the punishment in this subterranean world to be allowed, on rare occasions, to sit at table with the Emperor and to watch him drink his wine and from time to time be allowed a bone to crack?

For all the brutal strength and beastliness of Hyena that rose to the surface whenever he was away from his lord, he became in his presence transmuted into something weak and slavering. And Goat, whose personality was so overpowered by Hyena whenever they met above ground, was able, under the different conditions, to be quite another creature. The white and fierce grimace which was the Goat's interpretation of a smile was a more or less permanent feature of his long, dusty face. His sidelong walk became almost aggressive, for it was now combined with a kind of swagger; and he swung his arms about more freely under the impression that the more the cuffs were able to be seen the more genteel the wearer.

But this jauntiness was always a thing with a short life, for there lay at the back of everything the sinister presence of their dazzling lord.

White. White as the foam when the moon is full on the sea; white as the white of a child's eye; or the brow of a dead man; white as a sheeted ghost: oh, white as *wool*. Bright wool . . . white wool . . . in half a million curls . . . seraphic in its purity and softness . . . the raiment of the Lamb.

And all about it swam the darkness that shifted to the flicker of the candle flames.

For it was a great vault of solemn proportions: a place yawning with silence so that the movement of the little flames was almost like the sound of voices. But there were no animals or insects or birds or even vegetation to make any noise, nothing at all, except for the Lord of the Mines, lord of the unworked galleries and of a region deep in the body of the metal. He made no noise. He sat very softly and patiently in a high chair. Immediately before him was a table covered with a cloth of exquisite embroidery. The carpet on which the table was standing was thick and soft and of a very deep blood-red. Here, lost in the nether gloom, the lack of colour in the world above became changed into something that was not merely huelessness but was more than just colour; it was, for reason of the candles and the lamps, a kind of vivid stain; almost as though the lit objects burnt – or gave out, rather than absorbed, the light.

But the colours seemed to have no effect upon the Lamb, whose wool reflected nothing but itself and in one other particular, and that was in the matter of the eyes. The pupils were veiled with a dull blue membrane. This blue, dim as it was, had nevertheless a disproportionate effect, for the surrounding features were so angelically white. Set in this exquisite head, the eyes were like two coins.

The Lamb sat very upright, his white hands folded together in his lap. They were exquisite, like the hands of a child, for they were not only tiny but plump.

It was hard to believe in the primordial ages that lay beneath the down of those white hands. There they were, folded one about the other as though they loved one another; neither gripping one another too passionately, for they were made to be bruised, nor touching one another too lightly, for fear of losing the sweet palpation.

The breast of the lamb was like a little sea – a little sea of curls – of clustered curls or like the soft white crests of moonlight verdure; verdure white as death, frozen to the eye but voluptuously soft to the touch – and lethal also, for to plunge the hand into that breast would be to find there was no substance there but only the curls of the Lamb – no ribs, no organs; only the yielding, horrible mollience of endless wool.

And there was no heart to be found or to be heard. An ear laid to that deadly breast could hear nothing but a great silence, a wilderness of nothing; an infinite emptiness. And in the silence the two hands separated for a little while and then the fingertips touched one another in a strangely parsonic way, but only for a moment or two before they fled once again to one another so that their palms rejoined with a sound like a far-away gasp for breath.

This little sound, so infinitesimal in itself, was, nevertheless, in the silence that surrounded the Lamb, quite loud enough to set up a dozen echoes that, making their way into the remotest corners of the deserted galleries, up the throats of prodigious shafts and, where the great girders and coiling stairs of iron, crossed and re-crossed, split into lesser echoes, so that the whole of this subterranean kingdom became full of inaudible sounds as the air is full of motes.

It was a place forlorn. An emptiness. It was as though a great tide had withdrawn for ever from shores that had once been loud with voices.

There had been a time when these deserted solitudes were alive with hope, excitement and conjecture on how the world was to be changed! But that was far beyond the skyline. All that was left was a kind of ship-wreck. A shipwreck of metal. It spiralled; it took great arcs; it rose tier upon tier; it overhung vast wells of darkness; it formed gigantic stairs which came from nowhere and led nowhere. It led on and on; vistas of forgotten metal; moribund, stiff in a thousand attitudes of mortality; with not a rat, not a mouse; not a bat, not a spider. Only the Lamb, sitting in his high chair with a faint smile upon his lips; alone in the lux-ury of his vaulted chamber, where the red carpet was like blood, and the walls were lined with books that rose up . . . up . . . volume after volume until the shadows engulfed them.

But the Lamb was not happy for, though his brain was clear as ice, yet the hollow where his soul should have been seethed with horrible sick-ness. For his memory was both sharp and capacious, and he could recall not only a time when this adumbrate hall was filled with suppliants of all shapes and kinds at differing stages of mutation and dire change but the individual characters, ranging as they did, down the centuries each with its idiosyncrasies of gesture, stance and feature; each with its peculiar formations of bone; each with its textures, its mane or its stubble; the spotted, the striped, the skewball or the featureless. He had known them all. He had gathered them in at will, for in those halcyon days the world was alive with creatures, and he had but to call in that sweet voice of his for them to run and cluster at his throne.

But those far, thriving days were dead and gone, for gradually, one by one, they had all died, for the experiments were without precedent. That the Lamb had been able to continue his diabolical pastime, even after his blindness had turned the world into eternal midnight, was proof enough of the quenchless vitality of his evil. No, it was not that the lenses of the eyes had become thick and veiled – it was not anything of that nature that had caused the death of so many – it was that he had *willed* them to become while they were yet men beasts and beasts while they were yet men. This he could still achieve, for he could feel for and comprehend the structure of a head and pronounce at once the animal, the prototype that brooded, as it were, behind or within the human shape.

For where the Hyena now advanced with his steep back and his arms and his shaven jaw, and his white shirt, and his hideous laughter, there had once been a man whose tendency of feature was towards the beast that now possessed so much of him.

And in the core of the Goat that was now sidling through grey undergrowth, nearer and nearer with every step to the terrible mineshafts of the underworld, there had once been a man.

For it was the Lamb's exquisite pleasure to debase. To work upon and transform in such a way that, through terror and vile flattery subtly intertwined, his unwary victims, one by one, ceased to have a will of their own but began to disintegrate not only morally but palpably. It was then that he exerted a pressure upon them of a hellish kind for, having studied their varying types (the little white fingers fluttering here and there across the bony visages of many a trembling head), he began to will them into a state in which they longed to do what he wished them to do and be what he wished them to be. So that by degrees the form and character of the beasts they had somewhat resembled began to strengthen and little signs began to appear, such as a note in the voice that had never been there before, or a way of tossing the head like a stag or lowering it like a hen when it runs to its food.

But the Lamb, so agile of brain, so ingenious, was unable to keep them alive. In most cases this did not matter, but there were some of his beasts who had become, under his terrible aegis, creatures quite superbly idiotic in their proportions. Not only so but they, having their curious interplay between the beast and human within them, gave him continued sardonic pleasure, as a dwarf provides diversion for a king. But not for long. The more peculiar were those who died off first, for the whole process of transmutation was of so occult a nature that even the Lamb found it impossible to know what it was that killed them and what it was that kept them alive.

Why it was that somewhere in his complex make-up the Lamb had not only an angry, acrid fire burning, like an ulcer, no one can tell, but it is true that the very sight of a human being caused the colour of his flesh to change. So that it was not only a diversion on his part to drive a human soul into the deep and to find in there its equivalent and counter-part, among the masks of the world, but it was a loathing also – a deep and burning hatred of all humans.

A long time had passed since the last death, when a spider-man cried out for help, curled up, withered before the eyes of the Goat and the Lamb and disintegrated into dust, all in a moment. He had been, for the Lamb, some kind of companion for those rare occasions when the Lamb was in a mood for company. For the Spider had retained the qual-ity of its brain which was an interwoven and tenuous organ, and there were times when, the Lamb sitting on one side of a small ivory table and Spider on the other, they pursued long intellectual battles with some remote affinity to chess.

But this creature had died, and all that was left of the one-time court was the Hyena and the Goat.

Nothing seemed to kill these two. They lived on and on. The Lamb would sometimes sit and stare in their direction and, though it could *see* nothing, it could hear everything. So keen was its sense of hearing and of smell that, though the two creatures and the Boy were still long leagues away, yet they could even now be heard and smelt distinctly by this white overlord as he sat very upright with his hands folded.

But what was that faint and unfamiliar scent that came floating to the mines along with the more pungent odours of the Hyena and the Goat? At first there was no change in the position of the Lamb, but then, though the white head tilted back, the rest of the body remained immobile. The milk-white ears were pricked forward, and the sensitive nostrils quivered with the speed of an adder's tongue or of a bee's wing when it hovers above a flower. The eyes gazed blindly into the darkness overhead. All about him in the darkest areas or where the lamplight gloated on the terraced spines of his library something quite different was at large; a sense of quickening. The inscrutable Lamb, who had never been known to show his feelings, had parted, for a moment, with his own nature, for not only had he withdrawn as it were his head upon his shoulders, thus accentuating the rigidity of his posture, but an all-but-invisible tremor passed over his blind face.

For the smell of life approaching grew keener every moment though the distance between the subterranean mines and the stumbling trio was still a matter of many miles.

The three of them, led by the Hyena, had by now covered quite a tract of country. They had left the motionless woods behind them and had reached a belt of desiccated shrubs through which they waded. By now the heat had gone out of the day, and the Boy's hunger was causing him to cry.

'What are his eyes doing, my dear?' said the Goat, pointing as he did so with what looked like a handless arm, for the long semi-starched and dirty cuffs reached far beyond the hands and fingers.

'Stop for a moment, Hyena, love. What he is doing reminds me of something.'

'Oh, it does, does it, you son of a green stench? And what would that be? Eh?'

'Look and see for yourself, with your beautiful, clever face,' said the Goat. 'Can you see what I mean? Turn your head to me, Boy, so that your betters can enjoy the full of your countenance. You see, Hyena, dear, is it not as I told you? His eyes are full of bits of broken glass. Feel them, Hyena, feel them! They are wet and warm, and look – both his cheeks are swimming with water. It reminds me of something. What is it . . . ?'

'How should I know?' barked Hyena, irritably.

'Look,' continued the Goat. 'I can stroke his eyelids. How the White Lord will love to readjust him!'

A vague, unformulated fear swept through the Boy, though he could not understand what the Goat meant by 'readjustment'. Without knowing quite what he was doing, he struck out at the Goat, but in his weakness and tiredness the blow was so feeble that, though it landed on the shoulder of the Goat, yet the creature felt nothing but went on talking.

'Hyena, dear!'

'What, you hornhead?'

'Can you remember far enough . . . ?'

'Far enough *what?*' growled the Hyena, his smooth jaws working like clockwork.

'Far enough *back,* my love,' whispered the Goat, scratching himself, so that the dust poured out of his hide like smoke escaping from a chimney. 'Far enough back,' he repeated.

The Hyena shook his mane irritably. 'Far enough back for *what* – you knobhead?'

'For those long seasons, those decades, dear, those centuries. Don't you remember . . . before we were changed . . . when our limbs were beastless. We were, you know, my sweet Hyena, we *were* once.'

'We were *what?* Speak up, you damned Goat, or I'll crack you like a rib.'

'We were different once. You had no mane on your sloping back. It is very beautiful, but it wasn't there. And your long forearms.'

'What about them?'

'Well, they weren't always brindled, were they, dear?'

Hyena spat a cloud of bone-powder from between his powerful teeth. Then he leapt without warning at his colleague.

'Silence,' he cried, in a voice that at any moment might have veered into that terrible mournful cry which in turn might have let loose the diabolical laughter of the insane.

Standing with one of its feet planted upon the Goat, for Hyena had banged him to the ground, 'Silence,' he cried again. 'I do not want to remember.'

'Nor do I,' said the Goat. 'But I can remember *little* things. Curious *little* things. Before we changed, you know.'

'I said, silence!' said the Hyena, but this time there was something almost ruminative in the tone of his voice.

'You are bruising my ribs,' said Goat. 'Have pity, my dear. You are too savage with your friends. Ah . . . thank you, love. Bless me, you have a splendid . . . Look at the Boy.'

'Bring him back,' said Hyena, 'and I'll skin him.'

'He is for our White Lord,' said the Goat. 'I will cuff him.'

The Boy had indeed wandered away but only for a few yards. At the touch of the Goat he sank to his knees as though he had been felled like a young tree.

'I can remember quite a lot,' said the Goat, returning to Hyena. 'I can remember when my brow was clear and smooth.'

'Who cares,' yelled Hyena, in a fresh surge of temper. 'Who cares about your bloody brow?'

'And I can tell you something else,' said the Goat.

'What's that?'

'About this Boy.'

'What about him?'

'He must not die before the White Lord sees him. Look at him, Hyena. No! No! Hyena, dear. Kicking him will not help. Perhaps he is dying. Pick him up, Hyena. You are the noble one; you are the powerful one. Pick him up and gallop to the mines. To the mines, my dear, while I race on ahead.'

'What for?'

'To have his supper ready. He must have bread and water, mustn't he?'

The Hyena darted a mean and sidelong glance at the Goat before it turned to the Boy on the ground, and then, hardly stooping, caught him up in his brindled arms as though there was no weight at all.

So they set off again, the Goat trying to forge ahead, but he had not reckoned with the long, loping, sinewy run of his rival, whose voluminous white shirt billowed out behind. Sometimes it seemed that one of them was flagging and sometimes another – but for the most part they ran abreast.

The Boy was too far gone with exhaustion to understand what was happening. He did not even know that he was being held out at full length by Hyena rather as though he were a sacrifice. One advantage of this was that the odour of the powerful half-beast was to some extent mitigated, though it is doubtful whether the Boy's state of collapse allowed this amelioration to be appreciated.

Mile after mile they ran. The sea of shrubs through which they had waded for the last several miles had now given place to a thick kind of silvery rock-face, over which the Goat and the Hyena ran as though they were part of some immemorial legend, their long, drawn-out shadows bounding beside them, while the sun slid down the sky in a blur of hueless light. And then, suddenly, as the dark thickened, they felt the first sign that the ground was dropping away and that they had come to the great terraces that led downwards to the mines. And sure enough, there it was, that widespread congregation of ancient and deserted chimneys, their edges glinting in the early moonlight.

On seeing the chimneys Hyena and Goat came to a halt. Why they did so is not hard to guess, for they were now as much in the presence of the Lamb as they would be standing before him. From now on every single sound, no matter how faint, would be loud in the ears of their master.

They both knew this by bitter experience, for in the far-off days they had, along with other half-men, made the mistake of whispering to one another, not realizing that the merest breath was sucked into the great flues and chimneys and so down to the central areas where they turned and twisted, threading their way to where the Lamb sat upright, his ears and nostrils pricking with sentience.

Masters in the art of deaf and dumb language and also of lip-reading, they chose the latter, for the dangling position of the Goat's white cuffs obscured the fingers. So, staring one another in the face, they mouthed their words in deathly silence.

'He knows . . . we . . . are . . . here . . . Hyena . . . dear.'

'He . . . can . . . smell . . . us . . . by . . . now . . .'

'And . . . the . . . Boy . . .'

'Of . . . course . . . of . . . course . . . My . . . stomach's . . . turning . . . over . . .'

'I . . . will . . . go . . . first . . . with . . . the . . . Boy . . . and . . . prepare . . . his . . . supper . . . and . . . his . . . bed.'

'You . . . will . . . *not* . . . you . . . hornhead . . . Leave . . . him . . . to . . . me . . . or . . . I . . . will . . . crush . . . you.'

'Then . . . I . . . will . . . go . . . alone . . .'

'Of . . . course . . . you . . . dust-trap . . .'

'He . . . must . . . be . . . washed . . . tonight, and . . . fed . . . and . . . given . . . water. That is . . . for you . . . to do . . . since . . . you . . . insist. I . . . will . . . acquaint our Master . . . Oh . . . my green . . . loins . . . My . . . loins . . . My terrified . . . loins . . .'

They turned and withdrew from one another, their lips ceased to move, but as they ended their conversation they brought their lips together, and in his sanctum the White Lamb heard the sound of the cessation, a sound resembling that of a cobweb crumbling to the floor or the step of a mouse on moss.

So the Hyena went on alone, carrying the Boy before him in his hands, until he came to the foot of a prodigious shaft more like an abyss than anything consciously constructed. And here, on the edge of this great well of darkness, he knelt down and, clasping his horrid hands together, he whispered: 'White Lord of Midnight, hail!'

The five words fell almost palpably down the throat of the herbless, lifeless shaft and, echoing their way netherwards, came at last into the orbit of the Lamb's reception.

'It is Hyena, my lord, Hyena, whom you rescued from the upper void. Hyena, who came to you, to love you and serve your purposes. Hail!'

Then came a voice from the abysmal darkness. It was like a little bell tinkling, or the sound of naked innocence, or the crowing of a babe . . . or the bleating of a Lamb.

'You have somebody with you, I believe?'

The little voice trilled out of the darkness; it had no need to be raised. Like a needle piercing its way through rotten fabric, so this sweet sound penetrated to the furthermost recesses of the Underground Kingdom. It reached, trill upon echoing trill, into the dungeons away to the west, where, among the twisted girders of red rust, the silent floors were noduled with a sea of purple mushrooms, dead as the ground they had once risen from. It needed but the stamp of a foot to bring them down in a great death of colourless dust – no foot, no gust of air, nothing had passed that way for a hundred years.

It penetrated in every direction, this voice of the Lamb's . . . and now it spoke again.

'I am waiting for your answer . . . and for you.'

Then, with a thin sigh like the sound of a scythe, 'What have you brought back for me from out of the vile sunlight? What have you got for your lord? I am still waiting.'

'We have a Boy.'

'A Boy?'

'A Boy – touchless.'

There was a long silence during which Hyena thought he could hear something which he had never heard before, a remote throbbing.

But the voice of the Lamb was as clear and sweet and fresh as a water-shoot and quite emotionless.

'Where is the Goat'

'The Goat,' said Hyena, 'has done everything to hinder me. Shall I come down, my lord?'

'I think that what I said was "*Where* is the Goat?" I am not interested in whether or not he hinders you or you hinder him. What interests me at the moment is his whereabouts. Wait! Do I hear him in the Southern Gallery?'

'Yes, Master,' said the Hyena. He thrust his head and shoulders so far over the edge of the abyss that it would seem dangerous to anyone unacquainted with his miraculous head for heights and his general agility in dark and precipitous places.

'Yes, Master. The Goat is descending by the iron staircase. He has gone to prepare the Boy his bread and water. The hairless thing has fainted. You would not wish to see him, my White Lord, until he has been washed, fed and rested. Nor do you want to see the Goat, that stupid crackhead. I will not allow him to irk you.'

'You are strangely kind today,' came the sweet voice from the depths. 'So I am sure you will do what I tell you; for if you do otherwise I shall have your black mane burnt away. So come at once with your exhausted friend and I will size him up. I can smell him already, and I must say he is like a breath of fresh air in the place. Are you on your way? I don't hear anything.' The Lamb had bared its pearly teeth.

'I am on my way . . . Master . . . on my way . . .' cried the Hyena, who was shaking with fear, for the Lamb's voice was like a knife in a velvet sheath. 'I will bring him to you now to be yours for ever', and Hyena, his legs and arms still trembling in spite of all their strength, began to lower himself and the Boy over the edge of the pit, where a chain shone dimly in the moonlight.

In order to have both hands free for swarming down the iron chain, Hyena had slung the Boy over his shoulder, where he moaned pitifully.

But Hyena cared nothing about this, for he had recognized a note of a different blend in the Lamb's voice. He still spoke as gently, as horribly gently as before, but there was a difference now. What it was exactly that gave Hyena the impression that the voice had altered it is impossible to say, for Hyena could only *feel* the change, and the feel of it was that of hidden fervour.

Indeed what cause there was! Any creature of lesser calibre than the Lamb would by now have been unable to control the horrid thrill of his excitement.

For a decade or more had passed since the last visitor sat down at table with him – sat down and saw the veiled eyes of the Lamb and knew even as he stared at his host that his soul was being sucked out of him. He had died, like the rest, the brain running away too sharply from the body or the body leaping like a frog in search of the brain, so that they broke apart, and, like the machinery of the mines, they died away into silence and emptiness of death.

What it was that kept the last two underlings alive even the Lamb did not know. Something in their natures or in their organs gave the Goat and the Hyena some sort of physical immunity – something, perhaps, to do with their general coarseness of soul and fibre. They had outlived a hundred powerful beasts whose metamorphoses had in time destroyed them from within. The Lion, only an age ago, had collapsed in a mockery of power, bending his great head as he did so, the tears welling from the amber eyes, to thread their way down tracts of golden cheek-bone. It was a great and terrible fall: yet it was merciful, for, under the macabre aegis of the dazzling Lamb, the one-time king of beasts was brought to degradation, and there is nothing more foul than the draining of the heart's blood, drop by drop, from the great golden cat.

Collapsing with a roar, it had, so it seemed, dragged down the night, as though it were a curtain, and when the lanterns had been lit again there was nothing there but a cloak and breastplate and a dagger bright with stars and, floating away into the unutterable darkness of the Western Vaults, the mane of the great half-beast, like an aura.

And there had been the Man, delicate and nimble, across whose face the Lamb had drawn his finger, so that he knew, in his blindness, by touch and a quivering in the air that he was pure gazelle. But he had died a century after, at the exquisite height of a bound, his great eyes losing lustre as he fell . . .

And there had been the mantis-man, the pig-man and the dogs: the crocodile, the raven and that inordinate fish that sang like a linnet. But they had all died at one stage or another in their transmutation for lack of some ingredient, some necessity for survival, which for some obscure reason Hyena and the Goat possessed.

It was a source of chagrin to the Lamb that of all the divers creatures to have passed through his tiny, snow-white hands, creatures of all shapes, sizes and intellects, he should find himself left at last with a couple of near-idiots – the cowardly and bullying Hyena and the sycophantic Goat. There was a time when his secret vault with its rich carpets, golden candlesticks; incense burning in beakers of jade and its crimson awnings swaying a little from the distant updraught of the

air-shafts – there was a time when this sanctum had been filled with his hierophants who, awestruck at the sight of such a place, peered over one another's shoulders (shoulders of fur, shoulders of bristle, shoulders of raw hide, shoulders of scale and feather) at their lord, while he, the Lamb, the creator as it were of a new kingdom, a new species, sat on his high-backed throne, the dull blue membrane covering his eyes, his breast sumptuous with soft and peerless curls, his hands folded, his faintly tinctured lips the most delicate of mauves and on his head, on rare occasions, a crown of delicate bones exquisitely inter-woven, bleached to a whiteness that rivalled the very wool that was his raiment.

This crown was constructed from the thin bones of a stoat, and indeed it seemed that something of the stoat's mercurial and terrible vitality had remained in the marrow of the filigree structure, for when the Lamb, out of the diabolical hell of its heart, discovered his own heinous power to hold a victim rooted to the ground so that the blood within the creature yearned for annihilation at the hands of the torturer, the heart pounding against its will, then was it like the swaying stoat with its upright carriage and its kiss of death upon the jugular.

And indeed the Goat had seen it in the Lamb; and the Hyena also. That mesmeric swaying, that upright back. All but the kiss of death. All but the jugular. For the White Lamb was not interested in corpses (though they filled the darkness with their bones) but only in playthings.

And all he had left was the Hyena and the Goat. Yet he still held court. He was still the Lord of the Mines, though it was a great length of time since he had worn the Crown, for he had given up hope of new victims.

Year after year, decade after decade, in this subterranean world of silence and of death nothing had stirred, nothing had moved, not even the dust; nothing but their voices from time to time, when the Goat or Hyena reported at close of day, recounting to the Lamb the tale of each day's search. Search: fruitless search! That was the burden of their lives.

That was their purpose. To find another human, for the Lamb itched for his talents to burgeon once again. For he was like a pianist manacled, the keyboard before him. Or a famished gourmet unable to reach but able to see a table spread with delicacies.

But all this was over and the Lamb, though he made no sign, and though his voice was so smooth and even as oil on water, was consumed with an exquisite apprehension, quite terrible in its intensity.

The Lamb could hear two voices, one of them proceeding from the gigantic funnel to the north and the other, a good mile further to the east, much fainter but perfectly clear . . . a kind of obsequious shuffling.

The other noise was altogether more imminent and was of course proceeding from the nearby shaft where Hyena lowered himself link by link through the darkness with the Boy slung over his hirsute shoulders. As he descended three sounds preceded him: the grinding and straining of the iron links, a slow panting in the beast's capacious chest and the munching of small bones.

The Lamb, in his sanctum, alone, save for the loudening sound of his henchmen, sat very upright. Though his eyes were veiled and sightless, yet his entire face had something about it that was watchful. The head was not cocked upon one side; the ears were not pricked; there was no quivering to be seen; no tension; yet never was a creature as alert, as vile, as predatory. Cold horror was returning to the sanctum: the throbbing horror of the will. For the scent in the nostrils of the Lamb had by now become more specific. The field of odour had narrowed, and it was now no longer a matter of conjecture as to what it was that the Lamb would soon be touching with his soft white hand. He would be touching nothing less than flesh entirely *human*.

He could not, as yet, determine such niceties as the age of the captive, for he was shrouded in the fumes of iron that spread from the long chain, and the smell of the earth through which the well-head had been bored, not to speak of the indescribable effluvia of the Hyena – and a hundred other emanations.

But with every yard of descent these varying odours detached themselves one from another, and there came the moment when, with absolute surety, Hyena knew that there was a Boy in the shaft.

A Boy in the shaft. A Boy from the Other Region ... approaching ... descending ... This in itself was enough to cause the very girders of the mines to coil and spill red rust-like sand. It was enough to start exciting echoes – echoes unparented. Echoes that cried like demons; echoes at large like ears among the shadows; echoes of consternation; echoes delirious; echoes barbaric; echoes of exultation.

For the world had forsaken the mines, and time had forgotten them; yet here was the world again: the globe in microcosm. A human ... a Boy ... something to break ... or to batter down, as though it were clay ... and then to build again.

Meanwhile, as the moments passed, and the Hyena and the Boy drew nearer and nearer to the sumptuous vault below them where the Lamb sat immobile as a marble carving save only for the flickering of his dilated nostrils – the Goat, away to the west, had reached the wide and empty floor of the mines and was shuffling along in that horrible sideways gait of his, the left shoulder always in advance of the rest of his body. And as he made his furtive way he muttered to himself, for he was full of grievance. What right had Hyena to have all the credit? Why should Hyena make the presentation? It had been *he,* the Goat, who had found the human. It was bitterly unfair: a hotness of anger burnt like a live coal beneath his ribs. The cuffs of his jacket shook and his tombstone teeth were displayed in what could be taken either for a grin or a threat.

In fact it was a sign of frustration and hatred, a rankling hatred, for this was a moment never again to be repeated, a moment of such dramatic importance to the three of them that there should have been no question of rivalry for favour.

Could they not have approached their Emperor, the Lamb, together? Could they not have held the prisoner, one on either side, and made their bow together and offered him *together*? Oh, it was most unjust, and the Goat beat his hands together at his sides, and a nasty sweat poured down his long face, on the damp bristles through which his yellow eyes shone pale coins.

So strongly did he feel all this that he now began unconsciously to think of the Boy almost as a brother in distress: someone who, because of his hatred for Hyena (and this had been obvious from the first moment), had become, automatically and by pure retaliation, an ally.

But there was nothing he could do, in his pent-up condition, save make his way towards the vault some short way from which in his own dank quarters he would – as a gesture, or a slap in Hyena's face – he would prepare his *own* bed for the Boy and stave his hunger and thirst with water and sour bread.

It was obvious that the Boy's need for sleep and sustenance out-weighed any other factor, for what possible advantage could there be to the Lamb to see the thing he had been waiting for, for so many years, in a state of collapse?

He would wish for an alert and sentient prey, and it was the Goat's plan to put this point to the Lamb himself.

It was therefore a matter of great moment that the Goat should make all speed to the sumptuous sanctum of the Lamb, and he began to run as he had never run before.

On every side of him, above him and sometimes below him, the derelict remains of iron structures spread out their wild and sub-terranean arms. Brandished in giant loops: coiling in twisted stairways that led to nowhere, these relics of another age unfurled their iron fantasies as Goat sped by, covering the ground with quite unnatural pace.

It was very dark, but he knew this track of old and never by so much as a touch did he disturb a fragment of the litter that lay scattered on the wide floor. He knew it as an Indian knows the secret track through the woods, and, like the Indian, he was ignorant of the great fastness that lay on either side.

There came the time when the ground descended in a slow slope and the Goat, still running edgeways-on as though all hell was after him, came to the outskirts of that central dereliction where in his vault the White Lamb sat and waited.

Even the formidable muscles of Hyena were tested by such a climb, but he was now no more than a dozen feet from the subterranean floor, where every sound was amplified and echoes shuffled from wall to wall.

The Boy was no longer in a faint: his head had cleared, but his hunger was keener than ever and his limbs felt like water.

Once or twice he had raised himself a little from the shoulders of the half-beast but had fallen back again for lack of strength, though the mane upon which he fell was, for all the oiling that Hyena gave it, as coarse and thick as tare-grass.

Directly he landed he turned from the swinging chain and fixed his eyes upon the outer wall of the vault. Had he gazed up the throat of the ancient mine-shaft he would have seen – for his eyes were as keen as an eagle's – a pin-prick in the darkness; the colour of blood. It was all that could be seen of the sunset, that grain of crimson. But Hyena was not interested in staring up at crimson pin-heads but in the fact that he was now within a hundred feet of the Lamb.

He knew that even his breathing was overheard by his inscrutable lord, and he was about to take his first step forward when there was a sudden trampling to his left and a dusty creature in a black coat slewed itself into the picture and only drew up when it was within a yard of its irritable colleague. For it was of course the Goat, the dusty-headed Goat who had, to Hyena's amazement, a grin upon his face, a real grin and no mere show of teeth. It was not long before he knew the reason, and had it not been that every sound that was made was loud in the Lamb's ear there is no doubt the Goat would have been savaged mercilessly, if not killed, by the merciless Hyena.

For, during the last part of the Goat's solitary flight through the galleries and girders an idea had come to him, born of his hatred for Hyena who had so callously stolen from him the golden chance of pleasing the Lamb.

Hyena, though unaware of the meaning of the Goat's grin, yet knew no good could come of its implications, whatever they were, and he shook with suppressed rage as he glared murderously at his mulcted foe.

Unshouldering himself of the Boy, who slid to the ground, the Hyena, using the language of the deaf and dumb – for the faintest whisper would have sounded to the Lamb like the cracking and hissing of a forest fire – made rapid signs to the Goat which told that he proposed at the earliest opportunity to hack him to death.

In return the Goat, who mouthed his words syllable by syllable with his purplish lips, advised his enemy with a horrid oath to do no such thing, and then, to Hyena's amazement, turned away and, facing the outer walls of the sanctum, lifted his mealy voice.

'Lord Emperor and ever-dazzling Lamb,' he said. 'O thou by whom we live and breathe and are! Sun of our nether darkness, listen to your slave. For I have found him!'

There was a sudden wrenching sound, as of strangulation, as the Hyena, lifting his long, mean head, strained, as it were, on an invisible leash. His blood had mounted into his head and his eyes shone with a red light.

There was no sound from the Lamb so the Goat continued.

'I found him for you on the dusty plains. There I subdued him, brought him to his knees, drew from his belt his dagger: threw it away to where it sank in dust as a stone sinks in water; trussed him, and brought him to the mine-head. There, lounging in the sun, I found Hyena. The muscular Hyena, the foul Hyena –'

'Lies! Lies! You slavering knobhead! All lies, my lord! He never even –'

There came out of the gloom a gentle bleating – a sound sweet as April.

'Be quiet, children. Where is this human youth?'

As Hyena was about to tell the Lamb that the Boy was lying at his feet, the Goat whipped in with his answer.

'We have him, sir, prone on the earth floor. I suggest that he is fed, given water and then allowed to sleep. I shall prepare my bed for him, if you agree. Hyena's couch is foul with filthy bristles and hairs from his striped arms, and white with powder from the bones he munches. He could not sleep in such a place as that. Nor has Hyena any bread to give him. He is so bestial, my ivory lord: so unspeakably vile.'

But the Goat had gone too far and found himself at once upon his back. Over him loomed the trembling febrile and muscular darkness of Hyena. His jaws opening to their fullest disclosed a crimson world walled in with teeth – which, as they were about to close with a crack like gunfire, were held quivering in mid-air by that flute-like voice again, for the Lamb was calling . . .

'Bring me the youth that I may touch his temple. Is he unconscious?'

The Hyena knelt down upon his knees and stared at the Boy. Then he nodded his head. He had not recovered from the fabrications of the Goat nor from the uprush of anger he had just sustained.

The Boy, who was wide awake, felt a kind of extra sickness and knew intuitively that above all he must pretend at this moment to be unconscious or to be dead, and as the Goat bent over to inspect him he held his breath for twenty long seconds.

The proximity of the Goat was frightful to endure; but at last the creature rose and called out softly in the gloom: 'Insensible, O Lamb. Insensible as my horny hoof.'

'Then bring him to me, my pretty wranglers, and forget your puny rage. It is not you or the sound of you that interests me but the human youth. I am very old and so can sense the youth of him against me; and I am very young, so I can sense his nearness to my soul. Bring him to me now, before you wash him, dress him and give him food and sleep. Bring him to me, for my finger itches –'

And then suddenly there came from the throat of the Lamb a cry so shrill that had the Hyena or the Goat been looking at the Boy they could not have failed to see him start where he lay as though someone had pierced him with a needle. It was a cry so excruciatingly shrill and so unexpected that the Goat and Hyena drew closer together for all their hatred of one another. They had never, down the long decades, ever heard their lord throw out such a sound. It was as though, in spite of his grasp upon himself, the Lamb was yet unable to control the emotional pressure that filled his milk-white body – and so this jet of sound sprang through the darkness.

It was a long while before the high-pitched echoes died away and the yawning silence returned.

But it was not only that the sound had been shrill and sudden: there had been something else about it. It was no mere matter of the lungs or the vocal cords. It sprang from the uttermost pit of evil – a spearhead, a lance, a forerunner of dire menace. All that the Lamb had hidden for long centuries had shrilled its way through darkness into light.

But the Lamb was outwardly the same and sat if anything more upright than ever, the only difference being that the little snow-white hands were no longer folded. They were raised to the height of the shoulders in a gesture almost of a supplicant or of a mother holding an invisible child. The index fingers, curving a little inward, suggested, however, some kind of beckoning.

The head was bent back a little on the shoulders and looked as though it might strike forward at any moment like a cobra. The veiled eyes in their dull blue opacity appeared almost to see through the membrane. The Hyena and the Goat came forward supporting the Boy by his elbows.

Step by step they drew nearer to the Lamb, until they came to the wall that surrounded the innermost sanctum, and when they were only a few feet from the heavy curtains that formed the entrance they heard a sound of bleating, so faint, so far away; it was like innocence or a strain of love from the pastures of sweet April.

That was a sound they knew (the Goat and the Hyena), and they shuddered, for it brought with it no more love than can be found in a vampire's tongue.

'Once I have run my finger down his brow'– came the soft voice, 'and slid it down the profile to the chin, then take him from me, feed him and sleep him. I can smell his fatigue. If either or both of you should lose him in the mines'– continued the voice as sweet as honey and as light as birdsong – 'I will make you eat each other.'

Under his mane the Hyena turned as white as the bones he gnawed, and the Goat heaved with a sudden abortive sickness.

'Come in, my dears, and bring your treasure with you.'

'I come, Master,' cried the gruff voice of Hyena. 'I come, O my Emperor!'

'I have found him for you,' echoed the Goat, not to be outdone; and as they pushed their way through the curtains the Boy, unable to resist the temptation, opened his eyelids the merest fraction and stared through his eyelashes. It was only for a moment, and his eyes closed again but he had seen in that short space of time that the abode of the White Lamb was lit by many candles.

'Why do you keep me waiting, gentlemen?' The unnaturally sweet accents floated from above, for the chair in which the Lamb sat was a tall, sculpted affair, a good deal higher than is usual. 'Must I tell you to lie upon your backs and suffer? Now then . . . now then, where is he . . . ? Bring me the mortal.'

It was then that the Boy went through his darkest hell of all: the long ache of his body, acute as it was, was yet forgotten or disposed of in some way, for he was filled with a disembodied pain, an illness so penetrating, so horrible, that had he been given the opportunity to die he would have taken it. No normal sensation could find a way through this overpowering nausea of the soul that filled him.

For he was getting nearer and nearer to an icy aura that hung about the face of the Lamb. An aura like death, gelid and ghastly – yet febrile

also and terrible in its vitality – yet all was contained and held between the outlines of the long inscrutable visage, for, even when the Lamb had screamed, the face remained immobile, as though the head and the voice were strangers to one another.

This long face with its vibrance and its icy emanations was now very close to the Boy, who did not dare to raise his eyes, though he knew the Lamb was sightless. Then came the moment when the little finger of the Lamb's left hand moved forward like a short, white cater-pillar and, hovering for a little while near the victim's forehead, finally descended, and the Boy felt a touch on his brow that brought his heart into his throat.

For the finger of the Lamb appeared to suck at the temple like the sucker of an octopus, and then as the digit traced the profile it left behind it from the hair-line to the chin a track or wake so cold that his brow contracted with pain.

And that was enough, that tracing, to teach the Lamb all that he wished to know. In one sweep of the finger he had discovered that he had in the darkness before him a thing of quality, a thing of youth and style; something of pride, of a mortal unbeasted.

The effect upon the innermost system of the Lamb must have been horrible indeed for, though there appeared to be no visible excitement in the way he got to his feet and raised his blind face to the darkness over-head, yet at that moment when he moved his finger from the Boy's chin, a kind of covetous and fiery rash spread out beneath the wool, so that the milk-white curls appeared to be curdled, in a blush from head to feet.

'Take him away at once,' he whispered, 'and when this coma leaves him, and when he is fed and strong again, return him to me. For he is what your White Lord has awaited. His very bones cry out for realign-ment: his flesh to be reshaped; his heart to be shrivelled, and his soul to feed on fear.'

The Lamb was still standing. He raised his arms on either side like an oracle. His hands fluttered at the extremities of his arms like little white doves.

'Take him away. Prepare a feast. Forget nothing. My crown: the golden cutlery. The poison bottles; and the fumes; the wreaths of ivy and the bloody joints; the chains; the bowl of nettles; the spices; the baskets of fresh grass; the skulls and spines; the ribs and shoulder-blades. Forget nothing or, by the blindness of my sockets, I will have your hearts out. Take him away . . .'

Without waiting a moment Hyena and the Goat backed clumsily out of the candle-lit vault, and the heavy curtains fell back heavily into place.

As usual after a session with their ghastly lord, the two half-beasts clung together for a little while after the swinging back of the curtains, and the presence of their dank bodies was almost more than the Boy could stand, for he was wedged between them. Their internecine feud was by now forgotten in the fearful excitement: for they were to be witnesses of transformation. Together they put the Boy to bed (if a mouldering couch can be called a bed), and they fed him from an old tin of mashed-up bread and water. There was something almost lovable in the way they watched him lift his head to the wooden spoon. Their concentration was so childlike.

For a moment before the Boy fell asleep he gazed up at the two strange nurses, and there flashed through his mind the thought that, if it need be, he could outwit them both.

Then he turned over and collapsed into a thick and dreamless sleep while the Goat, sitting beside him, scratched interminably at his dusty head, while the Hyena, an ulna between his jaws, munched away in the darkness.

After about five hours of watching over the sleep-drugged Boy the two sentries got to their feet and made their way to the candle-lit vault. There being no reply to Hyena's query as to whether or not they might enter, they drew the curtains softly aside and peered in. At first they could see nothing. The spines of the books that filled one of the walls gleamed in the gloating light. The sumptuous red carpet flooded the floor: but the high chair was empty. Where was the Lamb?

Then they saw him, all at once, and with a start of recognition. His back was towards them, and such was the vagary of the light that standing there he was beyond the range of two clusters of candles he was all but invisible. But a little time later he moved a little to the west, and they saw his hands.

And yet, at the same time, they did not see his hands, for they were moving so fast one about another, circling one another, separating, threading and weaving their ten fantastic fingers in such a delirium of movement, that nothing could be seen but an opalescent blur of light that sometimes rose, sometimes sank and sometimes hovered like a mist at the height of the White Lamb's breast. What was happening? What was he doing? The Hyena shot a sideways glance at his companion and found no enlightenment there. How could they know that such were the fermentations in the brain of the Lamb that they could not be endured a moment longer without the aid of the body; for there comes a time when the brain, flashing through constellations of conjecture, is in danger of losing itself in worlds from which there is no return. And so the body, in its wisdom, flies alongside, ready, by means of its own rapidity, to grapple, if the need arose, with the dazzling convolutions of the brain. What the Hyena and the Goat were witnessing was just this. The intellectual excitement which the Boy aroused in the Lamb was of just such an order, so that, as it mounted in intensity, the little white fingers, rising intuitively to the occasion, held, by means of their own agility and speed, madness at bay.

All this was lost upon the two watchers through the curtain, but this was not to say that they were too dense to realize that this was not the right moment for disturbing their master. What it was that he was doing they did not know, but they knew enough to realize that it was something out of their own crass realm. So they retired as silently as possible and made their way to the midnight kitchens and the armoury and the baskets of fresh grass and all else that pertained to the Feast – and began, though they had many hours in hand, to polish the gold plate, the Crown and the shoulder-blades.

By now the Lamb, having subdued the speed of his own thought, had brought his hands together, as though in prayer and was now draped in a black shawl.

The Boy slept on . . . and on . . . and the hours moved slowly by, and the silence of the great subterranean mines became like a noise in itself – a kind of droning as of bees in a hollow tree; but eventually while

Goat and Hyena, resting at last from their labours, sat and stared at the sleeping mortal, the Boy awoke, and as he awoke he heard the Hyena rouse itself and spit out of its mouth a cloud of white bone-dust. Turning his head, the Hyena scowled at his confederate, and then, for no apparent reason, he reached out a long, brindled arm and brought it down heavily on the Goat's head.

This thump, that might have killed a man, merely shook the Goat badly and to ward off the possibilities of the Hyena repeating the attack the Goat showed his teeth in a grin both ingratiating and beastly; though it was true this smile was to some extent shrouded by the cloud of rising dust that billowed up from the Goat's head.

The Boy half opened his eyes and saw the Hyena immediately above him.

'Why did you strike me, Hyena, dear?' said the Goat.

'Because I wanted to.'

'Ah . . .'

'I loathe your loose purple lips –'

'Ah . . .'

'And your hairy belly –'

'I am sorry they displease you, dear.'

'Listen!'

'Yes, my love.'

'What will the White Lamb make of him, I wonder? Eh, you knob-head? What will he be? Eh?'

'Oh, Hyena, dear, shall I *tell* you what *I* think? . . .'

'What?'

'A hare!'

'No! No! No!'

'Why not, dear?

'Silence, you fool! A cockerel!'

'Oh, no, dear.'

'What do you dare to mean? I said a cockerel!'

'Or a rabbit?'

'No! No! No!'

'Or a porpoise? His skin is so smooth.'

'So was yours before the bristles rose. He'll build a burning cockerel from his bones.'

'Our Lord the Lamb will know.'

'Our Lord will bestialize him.'

'Then there'll be three of us.'

'Four, you fool! Four!'

'But the Lamb?'

'He is not one of us. He is . . .'

'He is not one of us . . .'

Whose voice was that? Whose was it? It was not theirs and it was not the Lamb's!

The two half-beasts leapt to their feet and stared about them until their gaze fell upon the Boy. His eyes were wide open, and it seemed in the semi-darkness that they were as alert and watchful as the eyes of a tracker. Not a muscle of his face moved, but his stomach swam with fearful apprehension.

From the very first when he had been accosted by the Goat he had, bit by bit, been able to piece together a foul, fantastic and unholy picture. A peculiar horror seeped through the heinous place, but this he now knew to be mere background to a nameless crime. The scattered sentences; the word here, the ejaculation there, had made it all too clear that he was to be sacrificed.

There was, nevertheless, a chip of granite at the heart of the Boy. Something obdurate. There was also something in his head. It was a brain.

It is hard for a brain to work adroitly when the hands are swimming in sweat and the stomach is retching with fear and nausea. But with a concentration quite fierce in its intensity he repeated yet again, *'He is not one of us.'*

The lips of the Hyena had drawn themselves back from the powerful teeth with a bewildered snarl. The powerful body appeared to vibrate beneath the voluminous white shirt. The hands gripped one another as though they fought in deadly grapple.

As for the Goat, it sidled alongside its colleague and peered at the boy with eyes the colour of lemon peel.

'One of us? The idea is absurd, gentlemen. We know better than to trust that baa-lamb.'

The Boy crept nearer to the pair, his finger to his lips until, when he was almost touching them, he began to mouth his words in absolute silence.

'I have great news for you,' he said. 'Watch my mouth closely. You shall be kings then indeed! For you are characters, gentlemen: characters in your own right. You have brains; you have muscles; you have resource; and, what is more important, you have the will to accomplish . . .'

'The will to accomplish what?' said the Hyena, spitting out a patella so that it skimmed its way into the gloom like a coin.

'The will to accomplish your own freedom. Your freedom to be kings . . .' said the Boy. 'Ah, it will stand you in good stead, gentlemen.'

'What will?' said the Goat.

'Why, your beauty, of course.'

There was a long silence during which the two beasts looked narrowly at the Boy, a nasty light in their eyes.

The Boy stood up.

'Yes, you are very beautiful,' he said again. 'Look at your arms: brindled and long as oars. Look at your sloping back. It is like a storm, mounting as it rises. Look at your shaven jaws as strong as death – and your long muzzle – oh, gentlemen, are they not seductive? Look at your foaming shirt and your mane of midnight. Look at –'

'Why not look at *me*?' said the Goat. 'What about my yellow eyes?'

'To bloody hell with your yellow eyes,' mouthed the Hyena savagely as he turned to the Boy. 'What was it you said about "kings"?'

'One thing at a time,' said the Boy. 'You must be patient. This is a day of hope and wild revenge. Do not interrupt me. I am a courier from another world. I bring you golden words.

'Listen!' said the Boy. 'Where I come from there is no more fear. But there is a roaring and a bellowing and a cracking of bones. And sometimes there is silence when, lolling on your thrones, your slaves adore you.'

The Hyena and the Goat looked over their shoulders at the curtained entrance of the Lamb's sanctum. They were obviously embarrassed. But they were excited also and slavering, though what the Boy meant they could not tell.

'What a place to live in!' said the Boy. 'This is a place for worms, not for the sons of man. But even the worms and the bats and the spiders avoid this place. For this is a home for fawners, slaves and sycophants. Let it be somewhere free, somewhere splendid, somewhere where you, sir,' – he turned to the Goat – 'can bury your splendid head in soft white dust, and where you' – he turned to the Hyena – 'can cut a cudgel, yes, and use it, too. And ah! the marrow-bones for your fierce jaws – the endless marrow! And I have come to fetch you.'

Again the two excited beasts looked over their shoulders to where the Lamb sat like a white carving beyond the curtains, save for the dull veil across his eyes.

But the habits of many years are not so easily broken, and it was not until the Boy had gone into detail in regard to where he proposed to take them, and where they would live, and the shape of their golden thrones, and the number of their slaves and a hundred other things that they dared to mention the Lamb: and then it was only because the Boy, unknown to them, had trapped them into a confession of fear. He had not given them a minute to recover but had jogged their minds along from statement to statement, from question to question, until quite apart from impressing them with his rhetoric he awoke in their bodies the ulcer of insurrection – for they had both been badly scared by the Lamb from time to time, and it was only terror held them back.

'Gentlemen,' said the Boy. 'You can help me and I can help you. I can give you power in the light of the sun. I can give you deserts and green places. I can give you back what once was yours before he tampered with your very birthright. As for what *you* can give *me*. Shall I tell you?'

The Hyena came forward to the Boy with something more horrible than ever about the slope of his back. When he was very close he brought his long, shaven head close to the Boy's who could see his own reflection in the beast's left eye, and he saw that he was shaking with fear.

'What is it we can give you?' mouthed the Hyena – and then, quick as an echo – 'What is it, dear? said the Goat. 'Do tell your –'

He never finished his sentence, for the air became filled with the voice of the Lamb, and as all three listeners turned their heads in the direction of the curtains they saw them part and something trotted out from between them – something unnaturally white.

The long bleat had brought the bristles up vertically on the back and arms of the Hyena, and the Goat had become frozen where it stood. Something had been apprehended in that seemingly innocent note – something which held no significance for the Boy, for he had no experience of the pain that always followed. But for Goat and Hyena it was otherwise. They had their memories. They knew of it.

But one thing that the Boy *did* realize, and that was that the two beasts, being filled with the slime of abject terror, were of no use to him at all, but equally they were of no use to their master.

The Boy was not to know that the anger at the heart of the bleat had been awakened by the empty table. Where was the feast? The feast during which he had hoped to begin his conquest of the wholly human youth. Where were his abominable henchmen?

As he, the Lamb, came through the curtain with his head held very high and his body sparkling like frost he was at the same time listening with his ears cocked, his nostrils dilated, and at once came upon the scent of the Hyena.

Walking with the nimbleness and delicacy of a dancer, the White Lamb came rapidly upon them.

It was now or never for the Boy. Without thinking, he pulled off his shoes and slid soundlessly into the adjacent gloom; to do this he was forced to elbow his way past Hyena, and as he did this he saw that creature's knife, a long, thin, deadly yard of steel, and he plucked it from the belt of the beast, and the noise this made turned the blind gaze of the White Lamb full upon him.

In spite of his tiptoeing, not only out of focus but out of alignment with the veiled eye, yet the Lamb followed with a horrible precision the movements of the Boy. Then all at once he turned his long woollen head away and a moment later had followed the path of his blind gaze and was circling the two half-beasts with a kind of strutting action; and as he did this the two creatures collapsed into a kind of decay. They were already travesties of life, but now they were nothing more than the relics of that travesty.

For, as the Lamb minced about them, they gave themselves up to his superior will, their eyes yearning for annihilation.

'When I kiss you,' said the Lamb in the sweetest voice in the world, 'then you will not die. Death is too gentle: death is too enviable: death is too generous. What I will give you is pain. For you have spoken to the Boy – and he was mine from the first word. You have touched him, and he was mine from the first touch. You have spoken of me: and in the hearing of the Boy, and that is treachery. You have not prepared the feast. So I will give you pain. Come and be kissed, that the pain may begin. Come to me . . . come.'

At the sight of the two creatures heaving their collapsed bodies across the floor the Boy retched with a nausea of the soul and body, and, lifting the sword above his head, he moved inch by inch towards the Lamb.

But he had progressed no further than a few feet before the Lamb ceased in its weavings and turning his head to one side took up an attitude of extreme concentration. The Boy, holding his breath, heard nothing in the hollow silence, but the Lamb could hear the beating of their hearts. It was towards the sound of one of the hearts, the heart of the Boy, that the Lamb now directed his entire sentience.

'Do not think there is anything you can *do*,' came the voice, like a chime of little bells, 'for already you are losing your strength . . . your nature is drifting from you . . . you are becoming mine.'

'No!' shouted the Boy. 'No! No! you tinkling devil!'

'Your shouting will not help you,' said the Lamb. 'My empire is hollow and empty, so do not shout. Look, instead, at your arm.'

Dragging his eyes away from the dazzling ghoul, he screamed to find that his fingers were not only curled unnaturally but that the whole arm was swinging to and fro, as though it had nothing to do with him or his body.

He tried to raise the hand, but nothing happened, except that as he cried with fear there was a note in his voice he did not recognize.

The concentration of the blind gaze upon him was like the pressure of a great weight. He tried to retreat, but his legs would not obey him. Yet his head was free and clear, and he knew that there was only one thing to do and that was to break the spell of scrutiny by some unexpected occurrence, and as this idea flashed through his mind he bent down very silently and placed the sword on the stone floor; and feeling in his pocket with his right hand he felt for a coin or a key. Luckily there were several coins, and taking a couple he lobbed them high in the air. By the time they landed on the floor beyond the Lamb the Boy had snatched up the sword with his one healthy hand.

Down came the coins with a sudden clang immediately *behind* the Lamb, and for the merest momentary flash of time the intense scrutiny of the tyrant was broken, and a deadly weight of oppression fled out of the air.

This was the only moment: the moment when all must be done before the resurgence of evil. The clearing of the air brought with it for one split second the loosening of the adhesions in his legs and a vibrance to his foul left arm so that he sprang forward with no sense of being retarded. In fact the air seemed to open up for him as he sprang, his sword brandished. He brought it down across the skull of the Lamb so that it split the head into two pieces which fell down on either side. There was no blood, nor anything to be seen in the nature of a brain.

The Boy then slashed at the woollen body and at the arms, but it was the same as it had been with the head, a complete emptiness devoid of bones and organs. The wool lay everywhere in dazzling curls.

The Boy sank to his knees, the relics of the white beast spread about him as though he had been shearing a sheep rather than slaying one.

Out of the intense darkness where Hyena and the Goat had crouched in subjection before their lord, two ancient men emerged. One had a sloping back, the other a sidelong shuffle. They did not talk to one another: they did not talk to the Boy, nor he to them. They led the way along cold galleries; through arches and up the throats of shafts until, in the upper air, they parted without a word.

The Boy was lost for a long while but, walking in a kind of dream, came eventually to the banks of a wide river where innumerable hounds awaited him. He boarded a little boat and was pushed across the water by the swimming pack, and by the time the boat touched ground on the far side his adventure had melted from his mind.

It was not long before one of a host of searchers found him lost and weary in a crumbling courtyard and carried him back to his immemorial home.

The Weird Journey

ONCE UPON A time-theory, when alone on the great bed, I found that no sooner had my head left the pillow than I fell wide awake. How far I fell I cannot say, but the light was brilliant all about me and the shrill cries of birds were loud in my ears – so loud, they seemed, that I could not tell whether they were in my brain or whether, all around my head and limbs, they spiralled in a flight too fleet for vision.

I could remember nothing save that I had come out of darkness – a kindly, muffling darkness, a daylight darkness, a summer of sepia, and that I was now in brilliance, the brilliance of night, very thrilling to the bones, where everything seemed diamond clear and *close*, frighteningly close, and palpable, stereoscopic and edged, and a kind of dye-like lucency coloured the merest grain of rock – the smallest frond.

I could not tell what size I was at first, but a sensation of height pervaded me, and glancing downwards it was not easy at first sight to perceive what footwear I favoured, though not a cloud lay between my head and a brand new pair of snakeskin striding boots. Not only were they of the stoutest and most brilliant snakeskin, but the speed at which they crossed one another startled me, for it was obvious that they were bound upon some journey with a purpose most immediate. I had no more idea of where they were going than I had of why my hands were raised and my fingertips joined and directed forwards at the level of my heart like a prow of a ship. But I knew well enough that to try to stay my progress would be futile, for I was on my way. Where? I did not know. Nor did I, at this juncture, care. Enough, it seemed to me, that I was on my way, after years of stillness.

I lifted my eyes from the deft and purposeful progress of my snake-skin covered feet and turned my attention to my other garments, which were, wherever possible, swept out in stiff horizontal flight, the two tails of my tie for instance, parting at the knot, flew over either shoulder like pennants, and my jacket, black and tarnished though it was, spread like the wings of some great fowl behind me – some fowl of hell, the state of whose matted nest (no doubt within the whorled throat of some blood-patched pinnacle) I shuddered to dwell upon. But what did it matter – sinister as was my flying jacket, it could not harm me, and I never so much as glanced over my shoulder a second time but turned my eyes to what lay ahead and about me.

I had no sensation of speed, though objects sped by me, less swiftly upon my right hand than upon my left, it is true, but very swiftly indeed for all that – and most speedily of all above my head where parrots tore past with bibles in their beaks.

One after another they flooded past, red, orange, yellow, green, blue, indigo, violet, in that order of rotation, the leaves of Genesis fluttering in the beak of the scarlet bird, Leviticus in the next and so on to Joshua, after which the wild story of Eden would again rattle its green pages in my ear as it sped by, and I closed my eyes for a few moments while my feet paced on. After a while I was able to open my eyes and take no notice at all of the spectrum birds, save when occasionally all the parrots would open their murderous beaks and cry 'Amen', shutting their mouths again with a clang before the bibles could overbalance and fall fluttering. But even this I grew used to, and I was able to concentrate on what lay further afield.

On my right-hand a green ocean, somewhat the colour of an unripe

apple, coughed and sneezed. The sands along its margin were covered with innumerable deckchairs, the canvas of each dyed in uniform stripes of red and white. Very neat they were, very clean – in groups, or aloof as they favoured. But no one sat in them, nor was anyone to be seen on that wide, clear strand. As far as eye could see little circles of foam slid about the feet of the most seaward chairs.

On my left, a grey mountain range was dotted with prawn-coloured villas, each one a replica of its neighbour. In the garden of every villa sat something that was smoking a pipe. I turned my head away quickly.

Ahead of me was the road that I travelled. It was cold and deathly white with artificial snow, and it was then that I noticed a most peculiar thing. Observing that in the distance the white road was speckled down its centre, I dropped my eyes gradually until, as my vision approached my own feet, I realized that I was looking at footprints. They rushed to meet me, or so it seemed, down the long strip of artificial snow, and as I was propelled forward and over them I found that my feet fell unerringly into their shallow, fish-shaped basins. Try as I would, I could not evade them. Footstep after footstep fell as though pre-ordained into its place. I tried to leap sideways, but a kind of magnetism drew the swift soles of my snakeskin boots into the flying footprints. But this was not all. Peering at each in turn, immediately before the descent of my either foot into its basin, I could see that the footprints were *mine*, the little snakeskin scales showing their imprints in the pressed snow. There was no doubt of it – let alone the simpler proof that my feet, long, slender and pidgeon-toed, had no duplicates – nor indeed any rivals among the feet of the world.

I could not escape the answer. I trod upon myself, upon my past; my early days; upon my childhood when I journeyed down white roads of wonder and innocence that were like the echoes of things long known and temporarily forgotten. But that was all very well. My childhood had not been like that. It had been surrounded by high grey acres of wallpaper and photographs gone yellow of marriage groups and dogs' heads and faded cricket teams. And huge aunts sat bolt upright in the corners of half-lit rooms and filled them up, and uncles stumbled across halls with guns under their arms, trailing their gammy legs. And I had been a wicked child. There had been no snow-white wonder or innocence about me. On the contrary I had made everyone irritated – and there was nothing strange, that I could remember, to account for this experience. Everything had been so very ordinary – with the great walnut tree outside the nursery window, with the white broken branch caught and kept from falling among the green leaves. And I was greedy – and my parents were weak and everything was very dreary. What had all this got to do with these footprints I trod in – these relics of myself? I could find no answer.

I began to be irritated by the way in which my body was propelling itself forward in complete disregard to any objective. It is absurd enough to find yourself on your way somewhere or another without wishing to reach any such place, but to travel like an automaton to an *unknown* destination appeared to me to be unhealthy and ludicrous. I had lost all interest in the fact that it was strange, for it was no longer so but hideously dreary.

My legs evidently had more moral power and vision than I had myself, and for a moment I flamed into a sudden temper and would have stamped the very feet that bore me had I been able to control them. I began to hate them. That there were two of them angered me. The mere fact that the very principle of perambulation necessitated a couple of feet held little weight with me. Two feet were twice as annoying as one when they travelled of their own volition and had me in their power and propelled me onwards in a nameless land. And then I began to be frightened – a nameless land. It was the words which frightened me more than the circumstance – and I began to shake as I walked and my mind began to be horrified at the possibilities which this progress opened up.

Suppose that I were taken to the verge of some precipice and were compelled to walk out into space . . . Suppose that they took me to some sharp den of fangs – or to some midnight cellar full of splashing water where the backs of soft beasts rose intermittently above the cold surface and occasionally some wet and yellow head that mewed and sank again . . .

Or suppose that my feet took me to some vast hall full of desks and carried me to the only empty one – hacked and scored by decades of penknife wounds, mutilated by the initials of whipped boys who could not understand their algebra . . . who wept and suffered from the horror and the whirling of algebraic symbols. . . who were ill because of algebra and died of it; while at the end of the great hall the master, whose face had no features, turned his blank mask at me, so that my wrists and forehead sweated with fear and my inky hand could not hold the slippery pen, and the algebra danced about the paper like flies on a window-pane . . .

Or supposing my feet took me into a land of whiteness where no colours could breathe and that I screamed for colour but none came; only whiteness like a theory, draining the love from life.

I struck my head to kill the fear that now possessed me, and in an effort to distract my mind I looked to left and right. But the deckchairs were still standing in their thousands by the sea. The long endless sands curved over the horizon. The foam still circled the legs of the most sea-ward chairs – there were no seagulls, but the sea was still bright and the coughing and sneezing of its million little waves sounded thinly and very far away – very forlorn – and terrible – for where were the spades, the sand castles, and the bathing huts and donkeys, the aunts and ugly women, the kites and the children? Oh, far away – far away, in some holiday from school – when, if heartache were mine, I could no longer recall it.

And on my left the range of grey mountains and the pink villas, but I turned my head away quickly, for fear of seeing the things in the gardens with pipes in their mouths. I longed for death, I ached and prayed for all volition to cease – for the unutterable consummation of final atrophy.

And yet, how weird it was, I felt no fatigue. My snakeskin boots flew on beneath me, and my body was light as a breath of air. And then it was that having turned my head away for some time from the landscape on my left, and the seascape on my right, a sense of uneasiness over and above my agony caused me to turn my head again to the ocean, for it seemed as though a memory of what I had seen disturbed me, yet I could not remember what it was. But I could see at once what had affected me, though my eyes had taken no message to my brain when last they saw the surf. It was nearer. It was drawing in. But not only the waves but the deckchairs also. Swinging my head to the left I found what I expected: the mountains with their pink villas were also approaching – the distance narrowing between the hills and the sea, until it seemed that in a few moments the deckchairs would be among the gardens of the villas and the things that smoked their pipes knee-deep in salt water – and the waves splashing their way up and over the neat green lawns and into the parlours of the prawn-coloured houses.

But the road of artificial snow was yet before me, when suddenly the footprints ceased to fly forwards and I was jolted into a spasm of rigidity and silence and the sky came down like a sheet of lead with a yellow circle painted in its centre. And the yellow circle came down with the sky in a dead weight, and striking my head the sun lost all its weight and all its shape for it melted and trickled over my face, and shoulders, a soft petal of fire, like a blob of honey settling into a fold of my sleeve.

And then again the cry of the parrots was heard – 'Amen! Amen! Amen!' and the pages of Deuteronomy fluttered over my face, and as I lowered the lamp I melted into a dream of tranquil beauty, the white sheets of my bed, as cool as water, swaying about my limbs and sighing 'Your journey is over – so wind your watch. . . so wind your watch. . . so wind your watch . . .' and unutterably happy to find myself no longer fast awake I turned over in the great bed and fell wide asleep.

I Bought a Palm-tree

PERHAPS IT'S BECAUSE there is something wrong with my upper storey, for I am incurably romantic. *King Solomon's Mines* still haunt me. *Coral Island* and *The Blue Water Ballads* are all mixed up in my memory. *Treasure Island* and *Westward Ho!* lie tangled in a thrill of memory. Ben Gunn and Amos Leigh, Ahab and Crusoe – they are with me still in a tangle of fern and palm-trees.

Yes, palm-trees, for it was always the tropics that called me. The tropics that one finds between the thick cardboard covers of dog-eared and thumb-marked story books. The tropics as one *wants* them, not as they are.

But I was never rational, nor honest enough or brave enough to admit that all this rainbow-tinted world was as false as a carrot-coloured toupé. But that's what I am, and it is because of this that I made the gesture of defiance, that cry against the machine age that brought in its wake a curious string of repercussions.

It all started one morning on the island of Sark. There was something in the air that day, a spicy, balmy something, almost tropical in itself though heaven knows I was thousands of miles away from the isles of spices, humming-birds and turtles. But I breathed deeply and I longed. I longed. What for? I didn't know at first, but I knew it must be for something that was a part of my childhood. A symbol I suppose.

While all that was happening inside me, I found myself striding to and fro across the rough lawn in front of our house; and as I stood my eyes became blurred and I saw the long beaches of Sacrota and the tossing heads of palm-trees. . . and then my eyes cleared and I was back in Sark again and was staring at the centre of the lawn where there was nothing but rough grass.

It was then that I knew what I wanted. I wanted a palm-tree of my own – a real live palm-tree, to stand upright before the windows of my house, its fronds trembling in the soft air. That's what I wanted.

'What are you doing, John?'

It was my wife's voice, calling from the porch.

'What is it? Have you seen a ghost?'

'Oh, it's nothing,' I said. (I was, and still am, a habitual liar.)

'Well, you look mad to me,' said my wife. 'Come and have your coffee.'

By now the idea of having a palm-tree of my own burnt with a fierce and yet fiercer flame.

'Isn't there some famous nursery in Guernsey, dear?'

'What sort of nursery?' replied my wife. 'There's no need to go to Guernsey.'

'Nursery for trees and things,' I said.

'There's Green Fingers, if that's what you mean,' said my wife. 'It's a famous one. But do have your coffee. It's getting cold!'

Hoping I was not observed I turned the pages of the Guernsey telephone directory. I found the name of the botanical gentleman in whose luxuriant nurseries I had once been shown what green fingers could do if they tried.

Peering up I noticed my wife had been taking no notice of me. I was not sure that I approved of this, but it was what I wanted. I could not have it both ways.

Surreptitiously I lifted the receiver. The voice of the Sark exchange asked me what I wanted.

'I want a Guernsey number,' I said.

'Ah,' said the voice. 'I suppose you know that the *Merry Widow* is doing a return trip on Thursday.'

'Who are you phoning?' said my wife.

'And what's more,' added the exchange, 'there's a cow being slaughtered. I thought I'd tell you.'

'I want Guernsey 1010.'

'Who are you phoning?' asked my wife.

'Ssh . . . ssh . . . ,' I said.

My plans had already gone wrong. I wanted the whole thing to be rather dramatic, but the *Merry Widow* and slaughtering information had taken the crispness out of what I was doing.

I don't know why, but I had remembered during the day the effect that Coral Island had had upon me, long ago, in a small room where I read it, sitting at a window in the right-hand wall, I remember. It was at some seaside town I think – probably Weymouth but I can't remember. And all the morning I had been haunted by the perfectly remembered sensation of tropical excitement in that small seaside room. And then I thought . . . but I'll let you know what I *did,* which is simpler.

And then the voice came through – the voice of the horticulturalist – the Man with the Green Fingers.

'Hullo.'

'Hullo,' I said and then in a very loud and commanding tone, much favoured by those who are mortally afraid of what they are doing, 'I want a palm-tree. Yes, a palm-tree. At once, if you please.'

I glanced up. It was a great moment for me. My wife looked quite definitely surprised.

'Certainly I can provide you with a palm-tree, sir,' said the voice. 'What variety were you thinking of?'

This was a cruel blow to me. This particularizing. It shook me at my

weakest point, which is my lack of general knowledge. How would *I* know what variety. I thought there were palm-trees *per se*.

I knew that to start a discussion as to the pros and cons of the various palm-trees in relation to the soil, the local weather conditions and so on would very soon show me up as the rank amateur that I am, not only in his eyes but, worse, in my wife's, and it was she whom I was determined to impress.

What I did I think was rather neat.

'I will ring you in half an hour,' I said and rang off.

Perhaps I sounded rude, but my status as a gardener was still intact.

'What is all this?' said my wife.

'Leave it to me, my dear,' I said. 'It's a technical business', and I made a dive for the encyclopaedia. The P to Plan volume had soon reminded one that the family Palmaceae was such a one as could put a Victorian ménage to shame for the prolixity of its nephews, aunts and brothers, nieces and grandchildren. I was reminded, or perhaps I should say I was *told*, of the Talipot, the date palm, the Palmyra, the ratten and cane palms, the Docem palm of Egypt. There were the feather palms Areca, Kentia, Calamus and Martinezia and the fan palms Latania, Borassus, Chamaerops and Sabal to name a few.

There were, I gathered, one thousand five hundred species, mainly tropical. This, I found dispiriting. I began to sweat. A kind of panic was on its way. The Chile coconut, or *Jubaea spectabile*, was to be found at its southern limit at 37° S latitude and the great centres of distribution are tropical America and tropical Asia, but tropical Africa contains only about a dozen genres though some of the species, like the doum palm (damn the doum, I muttered, my face pricking with the sense of my ignorance) and the deleb or Palmyra palm (*Borassus flabellifer*), have a wide distribution.

Like hell they had. I was sick of them already. But I grew pig-headed. After all I could not lift a receiver in front of my wife and demand the shipment of a palm-tree and then in a craven way back out of it.

The whole idea was to be sharp, matter-of-fact and, if you understand me, rather original and grandiose. It had deteriorated into something so confused and shaming that I knew that unless I acted quickly I would lose grip.

Sitting with the *Encyclopaedia Britannica* on my knee, I took a deep breath and lifted the receiver again.

'Hullo,' said the voice.

'Guernsey 1010.'

'Did I tell you about . . .'

'Guernsey 1010,' I screamed.

There was a deathly hush until suddenly the Voice of Green Fingers (how horribly controlled it was) cooed at me over the line.

'About that palm,' I said.

'Ah, yes.'

'I thought a *fan* palm,' I muttered.

'Very wise, sir.'

I sat up, feeling considerably better, and tried to find the place in the *Britannica*.

'Possibly the *Chamaerops humilis*, the Chusan palm, er, half a minute – or that Chilean thing, but what would you suggest?' I added in a rush.

'Would you care to leave it to me, sir?'

Damn the man. How could he have known I had my eye on the book.

'Very well,' I said rather grudgingly but secretly most relieved.

'And as to the size of leg, sir?'

'What sort of leg?'

There was a considerable silence.

'The bole,' he said, 'or trunk.'

'Do you mean what size tree do I want?'

'Exactly,' said the voice.

'The biggest you've got,' I said. 'How many hands would that be?'

'Our longest leg for transplanting would be about eleven feet, sir. I have a very decorative palm in mind.'

'Would it indeed?' I said. 'And can you send her right away?'

'Certainly, sir.'

The Connoisseurs

THERE WERE TWO men in the room, one a little plumper than he would have chosen and the other a little less upright. But both were fastidiously groomed. Their hands were very similar, soft and rather womanish.

'And what about that beautiful creature of a thing in that alcove?' said the less upright of the two.

'My poor vase?' queried his companion.

'Yes, yes, the vase. But, surely, very far from *poor*. Are the poor ever so elegant? I have been told they have their own kind of beauty – somebody told me that once – I don't remember who – don't ask me – but all the same, leaving the poor aside (as one usually does, God help us) – if you see what I mean – they are hardly *vases* – nor are they rare – my dear chap – one might say they are *never* rare.'

'And you think my vase so?'

'Oh, I *do*, I do indeed.'

'Strange ... '

'Why so ... ?'

I thought so, too. It cost me a lot of money. I was sure of it. I thought it was all right. It rang beautifully to the knuckle. It felt right. One might almost say it smelt right – though what could have less smell than a ceramic I can't think – but lately, and it is now many a long year after that first fine careless capture, I have begun to doubt it. I don't believe in it as I used to. Somehow it seems *wrong*.'

'Do you mean that you think it is a fake? Surely not!'

'I think so.'

'What! This beautiful creature of a thing?'

'I think so.'

'But look at its colour – look at its patina – look at its surface, look at its line, its ample girth and flow – Oh dear me, it can't be a fake – it just can't be – can it?'

'I think so.'

'Is there something a little, just a very little bit, too naïve about its neck-line? Something a little too studiously peasant-like in the handling of the shoulders – those sumptuous azure shoulders? Are they just a touch too ample for a master's hand?'

'I think so.'

'And the patina upon the crimson cranes – what do you feel? Just a shade too obviously encrusted – just a shade?'

'I think so.'

'Perhaps – perhaps. And yet how affected I was – and all for the wrong reason! I must watch myself more carefully – I really *must*. How curiously its glory crumbles off it. I see what you mean so exactly – there's a kind of *badness* in it – there positively *is*. You know what I mean by *badness*, don't you? As though the vase had gone off, as it were, like an egg, or like a tune that one has tired of – yet keeps its freshness – somehow.'

'I think so.'

'You are *right*. Oh, how right you are I can see it all now, so very, very clearly. The thing is a fake. Yes, yes, I can see that. In fact – it's ugly, it really is. It's a monster, ha-ha-ha! A red and blue monster! How can you, my dear fellow, have ever bought such a thing?'

'It took eight years, my dear chap, not eight minutes to arrive at *my*

suspicion. For eight years I have been torn between pleasure and distaste for the vase. However, there is only one way to prove my judgement.'

'And that is?'

'And that is to break it open!'

'To break it open?'

'To break it open and to make certain that there is no insignia the shape of a crab upon the inner side of the circular base. My doubt has made the thing hideous to me. Be good enough to witness the shattering of a fake and bloated beauty.'

'But –'

'Is this the moment for scruples?'

'No, no, my dear fellow . . . but . . .'

'But nothing – be good enough to pass me that poker. I thank you . . .'

'Are you quite . . . ?'

'Be quiet, please.'

'But what nerve – what belief in your own knowledge and flair, my dear chap. You amaze and startle me. It's magnificent. Here's the poker. I salute your intuition. Smash the impostor. Smash the gaudy thing!'

As the poker descended and the archaic vase broke open into four great leaf-shaped sections the connoisseurs went down upon their knees and found the insignia of the crab initialled in the unglazed clay, on the inner side of the vase's circular base.

It was genuine!

It was genuine!

It was beautiful after all!

Danse Macabre

WHETHER IT WAS the full moon that woke me I do not know. It may have been. Or it may be that the melancholy which had settled on my spirit and which coloured my dreams had become too strong for me to bear and had broken through my sleep and left me, of a sudden, aware and trembling.

It is no part of my story to tell you of the unhappy circumstances which had driven my dear wife away from me. I cannot tell you of that dreadful separation. It is sufficient to say that in spite of, or it may be *because* of, our ill-omen'd love, we were driven apart, though, as you shall hear, this desperate act brought nothing but horror in the end.

I had drawn wide the curtains when I had gone to bed, for the night was close, and now, with my eyes wide open, I found that my bedroom was filled with the light of the moon.

Facing me, as I lay upon my side, was my wardrobe, a tall piece of furniture, and my gaze wandered across the panels until they came to rest upon one of the metal door knobs.

Uneasy as I was, I had as yet no concrete cause for alarm; and would have closed my eyes had it not been that all at once my heart stopped beating. For the metal knob on which my gaze was fixed had begun, very slowly, very surely, to revolve, without a sound.

I cannot recall with any exactness what thoughts possessed me during the interminable turning of that brass knob. All I know is that what febrile thoughts I had were soaked in fear, so that my brain began to sweat no less than my body. But I could not turn my eyes away, nor close them. I could only watch as the cupboard door itself began to sway slowly open with hideous deliberation until it lay wide to the moon-filled room.

And then it happened . . . happened in the stillness when not so much as the call of a little owl from the nearby woods, or a sigh in the leaves, disturbed the small hours of that summer night, when my dress clothes on their hanger sailed slowly out of the depths of the wardrobe and with infinite smoothness came to a rest in mid-air immediately before my dressing table.

So unexpected, so ludicrous was this that it was a wonder I did not lose my nerve and scream. But the terror was caught in my throat and I made no sound but continued to watch as the trousers slid from the crossbar of the hanger until their extremities were no more than a couple of inches from the floor, in which position they remained, loose and empty. No sooner had this happened than an agitation at the shoulders made it plain that the white waistcoat and the long black tail-coat were trying to dislodge themselves from the hanger and then, all at once, they were free, and the hanger, leaving behind it in the room a headless, handless, footless spectre, floated into the depths of the cupboard and the door closed upon it.

By now the limp arms, for all their lack of hands, appeared in dumb-show to be knotting a white tie about a white collar, and then, most strange of all, the empty figure at the next moment was leaning forward in mid-air at an angle of thirty degrees from the floor, flinging the limp sleeves forwards as though about to dive, and with a whisk of the 'tails' it floated across the room and out of the window.

Before I knew what I was doing, I had reached the window and was just in time to see far away beyond the lawn, my dress clothes skimming their way towards the oak wood where they disappeared into the darkness beneath the trees.

How long I stood staring down across the lawn to the long dense margin of the oak wood I do not know, nor yet, when at last I returned across the room, how long I stared at the knob on the wardrobe door, before I had the courage to grip it and turn it and fling it open. I only know that at last I did so and saw the naked wooden hanger suspended there.

At last I slammed the door upon it and turned my back upon the cupboard. I began to pace the room in a fever of fearful foreboding. At last I fell exhausted upon my bed. It was only when dawn broke that I fell into a clammy sleep.

When I awoke it was past midday. The countryside was alive with familiar sounds; the squabbling of sparrows in the ivy outside the window; a dog barking and the drone of a tractor several fields across; and, listening half-asleep, it was a full minute before I recollected the nightmare I had suffered. Of course it was a nightmare! What else could it have been? With a short laugh I flung the bedclothes from me and got to my feet and began to dress. It was only when I was about to open the wardrobe door that I paused for a moment. The dream had been too vivid to be entirely disregarded even in the sane light of a summer day, but again I laughed, and the sound of my own laughter chilled me. It was like a child I once heard shouting out in his terror, 'I'm not afraid of *you*. I'm not afraid of *you*.'

Opening the door of the cupboard I sighed with relief for there, hanging demurely in the semi-darkness, were my evening clothes. Taking a tweed jacket from its hanger, I was about to close the door when I saw, clinging to the knee of my evening trousers, a wisp of grass.

It has always been a habit of mine, almost a fixation you might say, to keep my clothes in good condition. It seemed odd to me, this being so, that, having brushed my suit a night or two previously, there should be any kind of blemish. Why had the wisp of grass not caught my attention? However, strange as it seemed, I told myself there must, of course, be some simple explanation, and I dismissed the little problem from my mind.

Why I do not quite know, but I told no one of the dream, perhaps because anything strange or bizarre is distasteful to me and I presumed, perhaps wrongly, that such things are distasteful to others also. The memory of that horrible night lingered all day with me. Had it not been that I hate to be thought peculiar I think I would have found release in confiding the silly dream to someone or other. You see it was not simply frightening; it was ludicrous, too. Something more to smile about than to be afraid of. But I found I could not smile.

The next six days passed uneventfully enough. On the seventh evening, which was a Friday, I went to bed much later than is my usual practice, for some friends who had come to dinner with me had stayed talking until well after midnight, and when they had gone I began to read, so that it was close upon two o'clock before I climbed to my bedroom, where I sank upon the bed still fully clothed and continued for at least twenty minutes more to read my book.

By now I was drowsy, but before I got to my feet in order to undress I found that against my will I was directing my gaze at the cupboard. Fully believing that the dream had indeed been a dream, and nothing but a dream, the hideous habit had taken hold of me, so that the last thing I saw before I fell asleep was always – the door knob.

And again it moved, and again as terrible to me as ever before, it went on turning with the deliberate rotation, and my heart seemed to be stuck between my ribs, hammering for release in the silence of the second ghastly night. The sweat poured out of my skin and the avid taste of terror filled my mouth.

The fact that it was happening all over again, that it was a *repetition*, in no way helped me, for it appeared that what was once *unbelievable* was now an unarguable fact.

Slowly, inexorably, the knob turned and the cupboard door swung open and my evening clothes floated out as before and the trousers slid until they touched the ground, the hanger dislodged itself from the shoulders and it seemed there was no change in the absurd yet ghastly ritual, until it came to that moment when the apparition was about to turn to the window. This time it turned to me, and, though it had no face, I knew it *was* looking at me.

Then, as its entire body began to shake violently, I closed my eyes for no more than a second, but during that instant the clothes had disappeared through the open window.

I leapt to my feet and rushed to the window. At first I could see nothing, for I was directing my gaze at the lawn that stretched away for about sixty yards to the outskirts of the woods. No creature, ghost or mortal, could have covered that distance in the few seconds it took me to reach the window. But, then, some movement in the semi-darkness caused me to look down, and there it was, standing on the narrow gravel path immediately below me. Its back was to the house, and its sleeves were raised a little on either side, empty though they were.

Being exactly above the headless creature, I found that I was forced to see down into the horrible darkness of that circular pit whose outward rim was formed by the stiff, white collar. As I stared, nauseated, it began to skim, or glide, towards the lawn; it is hard to find a word that can adequately suggest the way it propelled itself across the ground, the tail-coat unnaturally upright, and the trouser-ends appearing almost to trail the grass, though they did not really touch the ground.

That I was dressed, I think, gave me courage, for, in spite of my inner terror, I ran down the stairs and out of the house and was just in time to see the apparition about to disappear into the woods beyond the lawn. I noted, as I ran, the spot at which it entered the forest, and fearing that I might lose the unholy thing I raced feverishly across the widespread lawn.

It was well that I did this, for on reaching the margin of the oak-wood I caught a glimpse of the high white collar and the gleam of cuffs away ahead and to the right.

Of course I knew the forest well enough by daylight, but by night it seemed a very different place, yet I followed as best I could, stumbling at times and all but losing sight of the floating thing as it flitted through the trees ahead of me. There seemed to be no hesitancy in its progress, and it occurred to me that, judging by the direction it was taking, it must very soon be coming upon the first of those long rides that ran from east to west across the forest.

And this was so, for it was only a few moments later that the foliage cleared above my head and I found myself standing on the verge of the long grassy avenue of oaks, and not a hundred paces to my left I saw my bodiless vesture.

Bodiless it may have been, but it did not appear so, in spite of the lack of feet or hands or head. For it became obvious that the garments were in a high state of agitation, turning this way and that, sometimes circling an oak tree on the far side of the avenue, sometimes floating an inch above the ground with the shoulders stooping forwards, almost as though in spite of its headlessness it peered down the long dwindling perspective of the forest ride.

Then, of a sudden, my heart leapt to my mouth, for my evening dress (its cuffs and collar gleaming in the dim light) had begun to tremble violently, and turning my eyes in the direction in which the suit was facing I saw, gliding towards us from a great way off, an ice-blue evening dress.

Nearer and nearer it came, nearer and nearer, floating with an effortless beauty, the long skirt trailing the ground. But there were no feet, and there were no arms or hands. And there was no head and yet there was something *familiar* about it as at last it reached my black attire and as I saw the sleeve of my coat pass itself around the ice-blue silken waist of the hollow lady, and a dance began which chilled my

blood, for though the movements were slow, almost leisurely, yet the headless thing was vibrating like the plucked string of a fiddle.

In contrast to this horrible vacillation, the evening dress of the other dancer moved in a strangely frozen manner made all the more horrible by its lack of arms. As I watched I began to feel a horrible sickness in my body and my knees began to give. In reaching for support I gripped a branch at my side, and to my horror it snapped off in my hands, with a report which in the silence of the night sounded like a gunshot. I lost my balance and fell upon my knees, but recovering at once I turned my gaze to the dancers. They were gone – gone as though they had never been. The avenue of tall trees stretched away in solemn, moonlit silence.

And then I saw what seemed to be a little heap of material jumbled untidily together on the sward. Steeling myself, I stepped out into the moonlight and made my way, step by step, towards the lifeless heap, and on reaching to within twelve feet of it I saw that it was composed of black material intertwined with a lovelier fabric the colour of blue ice.

I began to sweat where I stood, and I cannot tell how long I must have remained there, the sickness mounting in my stomach and my brain, when a movement in the untidy heap led at once to a further movement, and then before my eyes the parts began to disentangle themselves and to rise one by one from the ground and to reassemble in the air, and in another instant they were gone;  the lovely dress skimming the grass in the direction from which it had come until it dwindled to an ice-blue speck in the distance of the ride. My suit, no less swiftly, fled in the opposite direction and was gone, and I was left alone.

How I reached my home I shall never know – more, I think, by instinct than by reason, for I was feverish and deadly tired.

When at last I stumbled up the stairs and into my room I fell upon my knees and could not rise again for several minutes. When I did regain my feet I turned my gaze to the wardrobe and stared at the brass knob until a gust of courage filled me, and I turned the handle and the door swung open.

And there, hanging as primly as ever, were my tails and trousers.

During the week that followed I lived in a state of nervous excitement; an excitement most beastly. I was frightened, but I was also fascinated. I found myself thinking of nothing else but what would happen on the following Friday. The few friends I saw in the vicinity of my house were shocked at my appearance, for my face, which was naturally a fresh and ruddy colour, had turned grey. My hands trembled, and my eyes kept darting here and there as though I were at bay.

I told no one of what had happened. It was not that I was brave. It was more that I was cowardly. I have always had a distaste for the unearthly or anything remotely smacking of the supernatural, and I would never have lifted my head again in public if I knew myself to be regarded as some kind of metaphysical crank. I knew that I would rather go through this business alone, frightened as I was, than risk the raised eyebrows – the sidelong glance. When possible over the next seven days I avoided my friends. But there was one particular engagement which I could not avoid, nor wished to avoid.

I had promised, faithfully promised, to join some friends who were giving a small dinner party on the following Friday. But it was not just that – for if that had been all I would have invented some plausible excuse. No, it was for a very different reason. It was because my wife was to be there – our mutual friends, in their ignorance, were eager to reunite us. They had seen our illness mounting. For myself, my whole system was sick, for in truth I was but half a creature without her. And *she*? She who left me, seeing no hope for us but only a strengthening of that perverse and hideous *thing* that drives men to their own destruction, the more the love, the more the wish to hurt. What of her? Like me, they told me, those friends of mine, she also was sickening fast.

We were too proud to meet of our own will. Too proud or too selfish. And so this dinner had been cunningly arranged, and the time came when I arrived and was greeted by my hostess and my host and began to mix with the guests.

There was dinner and there was a little dancing, and, were I not to have been possessed, I might have enjoyed the evening, but my face kept turning to a little gold clock on the mantelpiece and from the clock to the door beyond the curtains that led to the hall.

As the evening wore on I began to suffer an absolute darkness of the spirit when suddenly she appeared and my heart gave a great bound and I trembled desperately, for though she was completely beautiful it was not her face I noticed first but the ice-blue of her dress.

We came together as though we had never parted, and though we knew that our meeting had been engineered yet there was suddenly too much joy in us for any thought of resentment to darken our thoughts.

But underneath our mounting joy was terror, for we could see in one another's eyes that we had suffered the same nightmare. We knew that, as we danced, our clothes were only waiting for the moment, two hours ahead, when some kind of dreaded thing would arrive and invest them with another life.

What were we to do? One thing we knew at once and that was that we must get away from the music and the gathering – a gathering which felt pleased with itself, no doubt, for we must have looked like lovers as we left the room trembling and hand in hand.

We knew we must keep together. But I also knew, as she knew, that if we were to break the spell at all we must attack; and end our role. But how? What could we do? Firstly, we must stay together; secondly, we must remain in our evening clothes.

The last hours before three o'clock were as long as all the days of our lives. I had driven her back to my house, or *our* house again, and we had rested there for the most part in silence. At first we talked of what it could mean, but it was beyond us. We had been chosen, so it seemed, to be the playthings of some demon.

We had all but fallen asleep when the first tremor swarmed my spine. Her head had been on my shoulder, and she awoke in an instant to find me rising to my feet, my body quaking and the material on my back and across my shoulders beginning to flap gently like a sail. Even in my horror I turned to her and she was rising also from the divan, rising as though drawn upwards with no effort, and, most horrible of all, there was a kind of blur across her lovely face, as though her features were less real than before.

'Oh, Harry,' she cried, 'Harry, where are you?' and she flung out her hand to me, and, oh, how precious was the touch of one another's fingers, for they had seemed to be no longer *there*, and by now our faces had *fled* also and our feet and our hands, yet we could *feel* the ground with our feet and the pressure of our cold palms.

Then there came to us the long shudder and the beginning of the *malevolence*. All I could see of her now was her ice-blue dress, but an evil of some kind, a malevolent evil, seemed to be entering our clothes – a vile restlessness, and we were torn apart, and from that moment I was never able to touch her again, or receive the blessing of her fingertips. And then, against our wills, we began to move, and as we moved together towards the windows I heard her voice again, 'Harry! Harry', very faint and far away, though we were quite close to one another, 'Harry! Harry, don't leave me.'

I could do nothing, for we were swept together out of the wide windows and without touching the lawn with our feet were flung to and fro in the air as though our clothes had but one object – to shake themselves free of us. There was no way of knowing how long this silent tumult went on. I only knew it was fraught with evil.

But, as the moments passed, there seemed to come a slackening in the violence, and though the sense of evil was in essence as vile as ever yet it seemed that the clothes were tiring. By the time they entered the wood they appeared to rest themselves on our bodies, and, though we heard nothing, it was as though they were gasping for breath or gasping for strength. It was as though there was the will to kill us but the means of doing so eluded them. By the time we reached the ride we were moving laboriously, and a little later we collapsed together beneath the oak tree.

It was almost dawn when I recovered my consciousness. I was drenched with an icy dew.

For a moment I had no idea where I was, but then the whole thing rose in my mind, and turning my head to right and left I found I was alone. My wife had gone.

In an agony of mind I stumbled home and up the stairs and into my bedroom. It was dark, and I struck a match. I hardly knew which way I was facing as I struck it, but I was not long left in doubt, for before me was the long mirror of the wardrobe. There facing me by the light of the match was a headless man, his shirt front, his cuffs and his collar gleaming.

Turning away in horror, not only at the sight but also the idea that the apparition was even now at large and that our struggle with the demons had been of no avail, I struck another match and turned to the bed.

Two people were lying there side by side, and peering closer I could see that they were smiling peacefully. My wife lay nearest to the window and I lay in my accustomed place, in the shadow of the wardrobe.

We were both dead.

Same Time, Same Place

THAT NIGHT I hated Father. He smelt of cabbage. There was cigarette ash all over his trousers. His untidy moustache was yellower and viler than ever with nicotine, and he took no notice of me. He simply sat there in his ugly armchair, his eyes half closed, brooding on the Lord knows what. I hated him. I hated his moustache. I even hated the smoke that drifted from his mouth and hung in the stale air above his head.

And when my mother came through the door and asked me whether I had seen her spectacles, I hated her, too. I hated the clothes she wore; tasteless and fussy. I hated them deeply. I hated something I had never noticed before; it was the way the heels of her shoes were worn away on their outside edges – not badly but appreciably. It looked mean to me, slatternly, and horribly human. I hated her for being human – like father.

She began to nag me about her glasses and the thread-bare con -dition of the elbows of my jacket, and suddenly I threw my book down. The room was unbearable. I felt suffocated. I suddenly realized that I must get away. I had lived with these two people for nearly twenty-three years. I had been born in the room immediately overhead. Was this the life for a young man? To spend his evenings watching the smoke drift out of his father's mouth and stain that decrepit old moustache, year after year – to watch the worn-away edges of my mother's heels, the dark brown furniture and the familiar stains on the chocolate-coloured carpet? I would go away; I would shake off the dark, smug mortality of the place. I would forgo my birthright. What of my father's business into which I would step at his death? What of it? To hell with it.

I began to make my way to the door, but at the third step I caught my foot in a ruck of the chocolate-coloured carpet, and in reaching out my hand for support I sent a pink vase flying.

Suddenly I felt very small and very angry. I saw my mother's mouth opening, and it reminded me of the front door and the front door reminded me of my urge to escape – to where? To where?

I did not wait to find an answer to my own question but, hardly knowing what I was doing, ran from the house.

The accumulated boredom of the last twenty-three years was at my back, and it seemed that I was propelled through the garden gate from its pressure against my shoulder-blades.

The road was wet with rain, black and shiny like oilskin. The reflection of the street-lamps wallowed like yellow jellyfish. A bus was approaching – a bus to Piccadilly, a bus to the never-never land – a bus to death or glory.

I found neither. I found something which haunts me still.

The great bus swayed as it sped. The black street gleamed. Through the window a hundred faces fluttered by as though the leaves of a dark book were being flicked over. And I sat there, with a sixpenny ticket in my hand. What was I doing? Where was I going?

To the centre of the world, I told myself. To Piccadilly Circus, where anything might happen. What did I *want* to happen?

I wanted life to happen! I wanted adventure; but already I was afraid. I wanted to find a beautiful woman. Bending my elbow I felt for the swelling of my biceps. There wasn't much to feel. 'Oh hell,' I said to myself, 'Oh damnable hell. This is *awful*.'

I stared out of the window, and there before me was the Circus. The lights were like a challenge. When the bus had curved its way from Regent Street and into Shaftesbury Avenue I alighted. Here was the jungle all about me, and I was lonely. The wild beasts prowled around me. The wolf packs surged and shuffled. Where was I to go? How wonderful it would have been to have known of some apartment, dimly lighted; of a door that opened to the secret knock, three short ones and one long one – where a strawberry blonde was waiting or perhaps, better still, some wise old lady with a cup of tea, an old lady, august and hallowed and whose heels were not worn down on their outside edges.

But I knew nowhere to go either for glamour or sympathy. Nowhere except the Corner House.

I made my way there. It was less congested than usual. I had only to queue for a few minutes before being allowed into the great eating-palace on the first floor. Oh, the marble and the gold of it all! The waiters coming and going, the band in the distance – how different all this was from an hour ago, when I stared at my father's moustache.

For some while I could find no table, and it was only when moving down the third of the long corridors between tables that I saw an old man leaving a table for two. The lady who had been sitting opposite him remained where she was. Had she left I would have had no tale to tell. Unsuspectingly I took the place of the old man and in reaching for the menu lifted my head and found myself gazing into the midnight pools of her eyes.

My hand hung poised over the menu. I could not move, for the head in front of me was magnificent. It was big and pale and indescribably proud – and what I would now call a greedy look seemed to me then to be an expression of rich assurance, of majestic beauty.

I knew at once that it was not the strawberry blonde of my callow fancy that I desired for glamour's sake, nor the comfort of the tea-tray lady – but this glorious creature before me who combined the mystery and exoticism of the former with the latter's mellow wisdom.

Was this not love at first sight? Why else should my heart have hammered like a foundry? Why should my hand have trembled above the menu? Why should my mouth have gone dry?

Words were quite impossible. It was clear to me that she knew everything that was going on in my breast and in my brain. The look of love which flooded from her eyes all but unhinged me. Taking my hand in hers she returned it to my side of the table where it lay like a dead thing on a plate. Then she passed me the menu. It meant nothing to me. The hors d'oeuvres and the sweets were all mixed together in a dance of letters.

What I told the waiter when he came I cannot remember, nor what he brought me. I know that I could not eat it. For an hour we sat there. We spoke with our eyes, with the pulse and stress of our excited breathing – and towards the end of this, our first meeting, with the tips of our fingers that in touching each other in the shadow of the teapot seemed to speak a language richer, subtler and more vibrant than words.

At last we were asked to go – and as I rose I spoke for the first time. 'Tomorrow?' I whispered. 'Tomorrow?' She nodded her magnificent head slowly. 'Same place? Same time?' She nodded again.

I waited for her to rise, but with a gentle yet authoritative gesture she signalled me away.

It seemed strange, but I knew I must go. I turned at the door and saw her sitting there, very still, very upright. Then I descended to the street

and made my way to Shaftesbury Avenue, my head in a whirl of stars, my legs weak and trembling, my heart on fire.

I had not decided to return home but found nevertheless that I was on my way back – back to the chocolate-coloured carpet, to my father in the ugly armchair, to my mother with her worn shoe heels.

When at last I turned the key it was near midnight. My mother had been crying. My father was angry. There were words, threats and entreaties on all sides. At last I got to bed.

The next day seemed endless, but at long last my excited fretting found some relief in action. Soon after tea I boarded the west-bound bus. It was already dark, but I was far too early when I arrived at the Circus.

I wandered restlessly here and there, adjusting my tie at shop windows and filing my nails for the hundredth time.

At last, when waking from a day dream as I sat for the fifth time in Leicester Square, I glanced at my watch and found I was three minutes late for our tryst.

I ran all the way panting with anxiety, but when I arrived at the table on the first floor I found my fear was baseless. She was there, more regal than ever, a monument of womanhood. Her large, pale face relaxed into an expression of such deep pleasure at the sight of me that I almost shouted for joy.

I will not speak of the tenderness of that evening. It was magic. It is enough to say that we determined that our destinies were inextricably joined.

When the time came for us to go I was surprised to find that the procedure of the previous night was once more expected of me. I could in no way make out the reason for it. Again I left her sitting alone at the table by the marble pillar. Again I vanished into the night alone, with those intoxicating words still on my lips. 'Tomorrow . . . tomorrow . . . same time . . . same place . . .'

The certainty of my love for her and hers for me was quite

intoxicating. I slept little that night and my restlessness on the following day was an agony both for me and my parents.

Before I left that night for our third meeting I crept into my mother's bedroom, and opening her jewel box I chose a ring from among her few trinkets. God knows it was not worthy to sit upon my loved one's finger, but it would symbolize our love.

Again she was waiting for me, though on this occasion I arrived a full quarter of an hour before our appointed time. It was as though, when we were together, we were hidden in a veil of love – as though we were alone. We heard nothing else but the sound of our voices; we saw nothing else but one another's eyes.

She put the ring upon her finger as soon as I had given it to her. Her hand that was holding mine tightened its grip. I was surprised at its power. My whole body trembled. I moved my foot beneath the table to touch hers. I could find it nowhere.

When once more the dreaded moment arrived, I left her sitting upright, the strong and tender smile of her farewell remaining in my mind like some fantastic sunrise.

For eight days we met thus, and parted thus, and with every meeting we knew more firmly than ever that whatever the difficulties that would result, whatever the forces against us, yet it was now that we must marry, now, while the magic was upon us.

On the eighth evening it was all decided. She knew that for my part it must be a secret wedding. My parents would never countenance so rapid an arrangement. She understood perfectly. For her part she wished a few of her friends to be present at the ceremony.

'I have a few colleagues,' she had said. I did not know what she meant, but her instructions as to where we should meet on the following afternoon put the remark out of my mind.

There was a registry office in Cambridge Circus, she told me, on the first floor of a certain building. I was to be there at four o'clock. She would arrange everything.

'Ah, my love,' she had murmured, shaking her large head slowly from side to side, 'how can I wait until then?' And with a smile unutterably bewitching she gestured for me to go, for the great marmoreal hall was all but empty.

For the eighth time I left her there. I knew that women must have their secrets and must be in no way thwarted in regard to them, and so, once again, I swallowed the question that I so longed to put to her. Why, oh why had I always to leave her there – and why, when I arrived to meet her, was she always there to meet me?

On the following day, after a careful search, I found a gold ring in a box in my father's dressing-table. Soon after three, having brushed my hair until it shone like sealskin, I set forth with a flower in my button-hole and a suitcase of belongings. It was a beautiful day with no wind and a clear sky.

The bus fled on like a fabulous beast, bearing me with it to a magic land.

But, alas, as we approached Mayfair we were held up more than once for long stretches of time. I began to get restless. By the time the bus had reached Shaftesbury Avenue I had but three minutes in which to reach the office.

It seemed strange that when the sunlight shone in sympathy with my marriage the traffic should choose to frustrate me. I was on the top of the bus and, having been given a very clear description of the building, was able, as we rounded at last into Cambridge Circus, to recognize it at once. When we came alongside my destination the traffic was held up again, and I was offered the perfect opportunity of disembarking immediately beneath the building.

My suitcase was at my feet, and as I stooped to pick it up I glanced at the windows on the first floor – for it was in one of those rooms that I was so soon to become a husband.

I was exactly on a level with the windows in question and commanded an unbroken view of the interior of a first-floor room. It could not have been more than a dozen feet away from where I sat.

I remember that our bus was hooting away, but there was no movement in the traffic ahead. The hooting came to me as through a dream, for I had become lost in another world.

My hand was clenched upon the handle of the suitcase. Through my eyes and into my brain an image was pouring. The image of the first-floor room.

I knew at once that it was in that particular room that I was expected. I cannot tell you why, for during those first few moments I had not seen her.

To the right of the stage (for I had the sensation of being in a theatre) was a table loaded with flowers. Behind the flowers sat a small pin-striped registrar. There were four others in the room, three of whom kept walking to and fro. The fourth, an enormous bearded lady, sat on a chair by the window. As I stared, one of the men bent over to speak to her. He had the longest neck on earth. His starched collar was the length of a walking stick, and his small bony head protruded from its extremity like the skull of a bird. The other two gentlemen who kept crossing and recrossing were very different. One was bald. His face and cranium were blue with the most intricate tattooing. His teeth were gold, and they shone like fire in his mouth. The other was a well-dressed young man and seemed normal enough until, as he came for a moment closer to the window, I saw that instead of a hand the cloven hoof of a goat protruded from the left sleeve.

And then suddenly it all happened. A door of their room must have opened, for all at once all the heads in the room were turned in one direction and a moment later a something in white trotted like a dog across the room.

But it was no dog. It was vertical as it ran. I thought at first that it was a mechanical doll, so close was it to the floor. I could not observe its face, but I was amazed to see the long train of satin that was being dragged along the carpet behind it.

It stopped when it reached the flower-laden table, and there was a

good deal of smiling and bowing, and then the man with the longest neck in the world placed a high stool in front of the table and, with the help of the young man with the goat foot, lifted the white thing so that it stood upon the high stool. The long satin dress was carefully draped over the stool so that it reached the floor on every side. It seemed as though a tall, dignified woman was standing at the civic altar.

And still I had not seen its face, though I knew what it would be like. A sense of nausea overwhelmed me and I sank back on the seat, hiding my face in my hands.

I cannot remember when the bus began to move. I know that I went on and on and on and that finally I was told that I had reached the terminus. There was nothing for it but to board another bus of the same number and make the return journey. A strange sense of relief had by now begun to blunt the edge of my disappointment. That this bus would take me to the door of the house where I was born gave me a twinge of homesick pleasure. But stronger was my sense of fear. I prayed that there would be no reason for the bus to be held up again in Cambridge Circus.

I had taken one of the downstairs seats, for I had no wish to be on an eye level with someone I had deserted. I had no sense of having wronged her, but she had been deserted nevertheless.

When at last the bus approached the Circus I peered into the half darkness. A street-lamp stood immediately below the registry office. I saw at once that there was no light in the office, and as the bus moved past I turned my eyes to a group beneath the street-lamp. My heart went cold in my breast.

Standing there, ossified as it were into a malignant mass – standing there as though they never intended to move until justice was done – were the five. It was only for a second that I saw them, but every lamp-lit head is for ever with me – the long-necked man with his bird skull head, his eyes glinting like chips of glass; to his right the small bald man, his tattooed scalp thrust forward, the lamplight gloating on the blue markings. To the left of the long-necked man stood the youth, his elegant body relaxed but a snarl on his face that I still sweat to remember. His hands were in his pockets, but I could see the shape of the hoof through the cloth. A little ahead of these three stood the bearded woman, a bulk of evil – and in the shadow that she cast before her I saw in that last fraction of a second, as the bus rolled me past, a big whitish head, very close to the ground.

In the dusk it appeared to be suspended above the kerb like a pale balloon with a red mouth painted upon it – a mouth that, taking a single diabolical curve, was more like the mouth of a wild beast than of a woman.

Long after I had left the group behind me – set, as it were, for ever

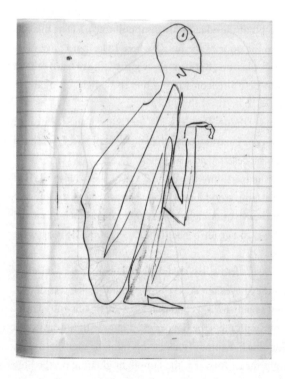

under the lamp, like something made of wax, like something monstrous, long after I had left it I yet saw it all. It filled the bus. They filled my brain. They fill it still.

When at last I arrived home I fell weeping upon my bed. My father and mother had no idea what it was all about, but they did not ask me. They never asked me.

That evening, after supper, I sat there, I remember, six years ago in my own chair on the chocolate-coloured carpet. I remember how I stared with love at the ash on my father's waistcoat, at his stained moustache, at my mother's worn-away shoe heels. I stared at it all and I loved it all. I needed it all.

Since then I have never left the house. I know what is best for me.

Illustration credits

The pictures on pages 12, 25, 102, 104 and 135 are reproduced by kind permission of the Chris Beetles Gallery, London. The cover illustration and other pictures in the text appear courtesy of the Estate of Mervyn Peake.

By the same author and available from Peter Owen

MERVYN PEAKE

A Book of Nonsense: Poems and Drawings Revised and Expanded Centenary Edition

978-0-7206-1361-2 paperback illustrated £9.99

With an Introduction by Maeve Gilmore

With Forewords by Sebastian Peake and Benjamin Zephaniah

From the macabre to the brilliantly offbeat, Mervyn Peake's nonsense verse can be enjoyed by young and old alike. This collection of writings and drawings was selected by his widow, Maeve Gilmore, and it introduces a whole gallery of characters and creatures, such as the Dwarf of Battersea and Footfruit. Quirky and comical, occasionally alarming, but always magical.

The volume is illustrated by Peake, and, in this new edition celebrating the centenary of his birth, twelve new previously unpublished drawings have been included.

'This book gave me permission to rhyme, it gave me permission to play with my words . . . It is one of the few books I always return to. This book is a masterpiece and a piece from a master.' BENJAMIN ZEPHANIAH

'Peake deserves a place among the eccentrics of the English tradition alongside Sterne, Blake, Lear, Carroll and Belloc.' TIMES LITERARY SUPPLEMENT

'He can try on the strangest clothes without losing his own strange identity . . . a genuinely haunted imagination which stamps everything he wrote or drew.' GUARDIAN

SEBASTIAN PEAKE AND ALISON ELDRED (COMPILERS)
G. PETER WINNINGTON (EDITOR)

Mervyn Peake: The Man and His Art

978-0-7206-1321-6 paperback illustrated £19.95

Mervyn Peake (1911–1968) was one of the most multi-talented artists of the twentieth century. Painter, novelist, author of children's books and nonsense verse, poet and dramatist, he also illustrated such classic works as *Treasure Island*, *Alice's Adventures in Wonderland*, *The Rime of the Ancient Mariner*, *Grimm's Household Tales* and *Bleak House*. A man of extraordinary vision and imagination, his literary and artistic creations – especially his Gormenghast trilogy – are unforgettable, and his influence is felt to this day.

In this volume, a stunning collection of illustrations, paintings, notebook pages and other material – much previously unpublished – has been gathered together and combined with detailed biographical information as well as tributes by writers and artists such as Michael Moorcock, Joanne Harris, John Howe and Chris Riddell and others to produce a unique memoir of Peake's life and work. The book includes sections on Peake's upbringing as son of a missionary doctor in China, marriage and fatherhood, his experiences as a war artist, the creation of his celebrated Titus trilogy, *Mr Pye* and other literary works, and his tragic decline as illness overcame him, resulting in his early death. This handsome volume is a must for art historians and all fans of Peake's work.

'*Mervyn Peake was an artist and writer of extraordinary originality and prolificity* . . . The Man and His Art *displays a genius of Gothic grotesquerie.*' PATRICK SKENE CATLING, IRISH TIMES

G. PETER WINNINGTON

Mervyn Peake's Vast Alchemies: The Illustrated Biography

978-0-7206-1341-4 paperback illustrated £14.99

Mervyn Peake's Vast Alchemies is the result of many years of research into Peake's life and work. It follows Peake, the son of missionary parents, from China to art school in London and his time in an artists' colony in the Channel Islands. It covers in detail his experiences in the army during the Second World War, an unhappy period during which he wrote *Titus Groan* and the huge influence that his visit to the newly liberated concentration camp at Belsen had on his work. The next ten years of his life were without doubt his most productive, but by the mid-1950s he was beginning to show signs of the degenerative illness that eventually killed him in 1968.

In this revised version of his acclaimed biography, *Vast Alchemies: The Life and Work of Mervyn Peake*, G. Peter Winnington examines the novels, poems, illustrations and plays and discusses how Peake's life and experiences were channelled through his unique imagination into his work. This new edition also features photographs, paintings and drawings specially released by the Mervyn Peake Estate.

G. Peter Winnington has edited successively the *Mervyn Peake Review* and *Peake Studies* and compiled a bibliography of Peake's published work. He is author of *The Voice of the Heart: The Working of Mervyn Peake's Imagination* and edited and contributed to *Mervyn Peake: The Man and His Art*. He also prepared revised editions of the Titus novels for Penguin.

'*By far the best biography I've read of Peake and the closest to the reality that I perceived.*' MICHAEL MOORCOCK

'*Peter Winnington could well know more about Peake than anyone else.*' INDEPENDENT

'*Succeeds very well in recreating the world in which Peake moved.*' SPECTATOR